Hey, Ha

CW00422468

Pre-Teens Solve a Murder on Their Doorstep

By Ann Boulting
©2011 Black Pug Publishing, Inc.

Dedication

To my wonderful son whose brilliance and guidance has been an inspiration to me always. A better son I couldn't ask for...

Table of Contents

Chapter I

The shriek brought Haydecker out of a deep sleep. She lay there in her warm bed listening, her heart pounding. There was confusion in the foyer, a wail of voices, a slam of doors.

The clock announced 6:07 in large, red numbers. With a flick of a finger at the console of buttons, Haydecker activated the huge drape covering the glass wall at the end of her bedroom. The morning had not yet come. A few dim stars glittered in a cold, dark, wintry sky.

She heard the opening of the apartment door and her mother's voice. The noise level was loud and then soft again. Haydecker pushed another button on the console and the TV screen flickered and then flashed its blue-white light to reveal the foyer of the seventh floor and a crowd of people standing around staring at the carpet. Haydecker could stand it no longer.

In spite of the lectures and the scoldings and the warnings, in spite of the aches in her joints as her feet touched the fuzzy TAZ slippers, she was going to see what was happening. Something was definitely happening in the foyer. The seventh floor was not known for large social gatherings at 6:00 in the morning. She pulled the warm red robe around her as she shuffled to the entrance of the apartment.

The crowd proved to be the apartment residents. They stood around the thickly carpeted foyer in nearly every state of dress, robes flung hastily on, curlers hanging limply from heads, faces half shaven. They shared one thing in common; the look of shock and horror was on every face. Haydecker could hardly wait to see. At the same time, she was afraid to look. She closed, then opened her eyes.

The center of attention was the body lying on the floor directly in front of the elevator. Long, blond hair lay fanned out on the dark green carpet. Haydecker looked closely for any movement. There was none. Haydecker felt a tightening in her chest as she guessed the reason for the stillness.

Some of the onlookers were babbling. No one was saying anything that made any sense. Haydecker carefully inched closer for a better look--but not too close.

She didn't recognize the face of the girl whose body lay twisted, her arms and legs akimbo on the plush of the floor. At least it wasn't somebody from the apartment building, from the Hatterfield Towers.

Woof crept close and stuck his wet nose into her hand. She jumped. The jump, of course, caught her mother's attention.

"Emily Marie, what are you doing out of bed? Go back to the apartment immediately." It was usual. A time of crisis and her mother would always give orders. Haydecker didn't get excited until her mother used all three of her names to order her to do something. This was the most exciting thing that had happened since she had been rushed in the ambulance from school. She wasn't going to miss this! She felt guilty about ignoring her mother but—not too bad.

Everyone's attention, including her mother's, was diverted by the opening of the elevator door. Two sleepy-eyed men nearly tripped over the body in their early morning daze.

The taller of the two was slat thin. When he knelt to examine the body, he folded like a piece of paper. In contrast, his partner had an extra roll of fat around the middle and let out a poof of air as he bent over to check for a pulse.

"She's dead." The plump man stated.

"Great start!" Haydecker thought to herself.

The talking and the shuffling had ceased. Everyone stood and stared. The two policemen stared. It seemed as if no one could think of what to do next.

The elevator doors plopped open again to reveal Mad Harold, alias Harold Simpson, the combination doorman and security guard for the building. He had come to take Woof for his morning walk. Mad Harold, whose hair was never very well combed, ran his fingers through the brown bush causing it to stand straight up. He, too, stared at the scene. Woof, grateful to see his friend, greeted him joyfully.

Woof was the only one who was joyful at the moment. Woof wagged a lot since he couldn't bark, being a Basenji. When Haydecker had gotten sick, the Towers management had made an exception for Woof. No dogs were allowed, but Woof really didn't count as he was a companion for Haydecker who was alone most days. Even Woof never really considered himself a dog, more like a four-legged person. That is if he could have counted. Haydecker was sure, quite sure, that sometimes he could. There were days when she was sure that Woof was her very best friend.

"Harold," Mrs. Haydecker, again, barking orders, "take Woof out, now!"

Harold, with effort, broke his fascinated stare and herded the dog into the elevator. His mouth was still open as the door closed while the police man growled, "Be sure you get right back up here, young man. We have some questions to ask you."

Mrs. Sylvia Haydecker wasn't through. "Emily Marie, you get back to bed." She took her daughter's arm firmly and they marched back across the foyer and into the apartment where she gave Haydecker a push toward the bedroom.

Chapter II

Emily Marie Haydecker bounced under the covers, and the electric warmth immediately eased her aching legs. She rolled over and punched another button on Wally's console. Wally was Haydecker's electronic companion just as Woof was her canine companion. Wally had been personally designed and built by Emily's father, George Haydecker, as a babysitter, nurse, teacher, entertainer and guardian. Woof got the watch-dog chores. Wally did everything but deliver pizza. Of course, he could arrange to have that done as well.

The punch of the button brought sound into her bedroom, the murmur of voices and the sharp voices of the two policemen. She brought the volume up on the intercom. She could see and hear the events in the foyer. It was like her own private movie. Except that this time, someone was really dead. It wasn't make-believe.

"Okay, folks, now let's move. Everyone go to their own apartments and stay there." It was the plump detective. Haydecker, for the sake of communication, dubbed him Chubb. The tall, dark detective became Silent Sam. He didn't say anything, but made flapping motions with his arms. Haydecker thought that Silent Sam would get on well with Woof. Both were giants in the conversation department.

Everyone in the hall moved back a step or two but no one made any effort to leave. Chubb tried again, "Does anyone here know who this young woman is?" And the group was more still and silent than before. Haydecker wondered how long even a death would silence Golda Heifitz.

Haydecker made a mental note of the assemblage. Golda Heifitz from next door in 7D; General Cargill, already completely dressed and shaven, from 7H; O. P. McCaw from down the hall in 7F looked as if he had flung on his great grandfather's flannel robe. Grace Onken, the school teacher from 7G was in a filmy blue nightgown which had its effect spoiled by the pink hair curlers; and both Sara and Dwight Mohr (or as Sara called him, "Dee Dee) from 7B in matching bathrobes, which were, Haydecker supposed, wedding presents.

Who was missing? Rose and Oliver Brower and their daughter Marcia from 7E; Sherry Gerot, Grace's roommate; and O. P. MaCaw's wife, Catherine and little ten-year-old Ozzie. Young Ozzie would really grit his teeth having missed a real live dead body. He would talk about it for days. Haydecker was glad she had risked her mother's anger to go out into the foyer for a first-hand look. It was worth it. She would be able to stuff it in Ozzie's teeth. She couldn't "one-up-him" very often when she had to stay in bed all the time. At least this event would break up the winter boredom of long days and nights for Haydecker.

Haydecker breathed a sigh at the near miss--at least, she had actually seen the body. Just let Ozzie get snotty about that! Ozzie sorely felt his junior status being three years younger than Haydecker and the youngest kid in the building. He never failed to point out, however, that he was free to come and go. Haydecker would just as soon have never seen Ozzie from one week to the next but he was the messenger from Pelham Private Day School and was in charge of delivering Haydecker's assignments to school. Haydecker grudgingly had to admit that, as a messenger, he was OK. As a mouth, Ozzie was obnoxious.

Watching the monitor, Haydecker could see the detectives shooing everyone back into their respective apartments. They were being again instructed that they should not leave the building until preliminary questioning had been completed. Someone had provided a blanket for the body and it had become a red and green plaid lump on the foyer floor. Haydecker thought that the blanket went well with the carpet.

The elevator opened to reveal Mad Harold and Woof, back from the shortest morning outing of their careers. Woof stepped gingerly off the elevator, his nose to the floor, and made quiet, snuffling noises. Harold still stood inside the door with his finger on the STOP button.

Chubb pounced, "You the doorman here?" The words were rather indistinct, but Haydecker, by turning up the volume to the fullest could catch most of them.

Harold nodded, his eyes riveted on the blanket.

"What time did you come on duty this morning."

"I go on," Harold stopped to swallow what sounded like a huge lump in his throat, "duty at 6:30 but I come here a little after 6:00 to walk the Haydecker's dog."

"Did you see this woman this morning?" Silent Sam whipped back the corner of the plaid blanket.

"Never saw her before." Mad Harold didn't look too closely, Haydecker noticed. Woof was getting braver though and was sniffing as he crept ever closer to Miss Plaid Lump.

"Get that darn dog back where he belongs and then you get out here." It was Chubb again barking the orders.

Mad Harold lost no time in grabbing Woof by the studded red collar and hustling across the foyer, half-dragging Woof who was, by then, reluctant to leave the proceedings. He was really beginning to get interested. Haydecker understood how he felt. It was the most interesting thing in both of their lives in a long time. Haydecker was sure that Woof minded as much as she did being stuck in this stuffy old room day after day.

"Hey, Haydecker, open up!" Mad Harold looked into the camera and punched the buzzer.

"It's open, Harold, come on in."

Mad Harold and Woof disappeared from Wally's television screen only to reappear in a moment in the door of the bedroom.

"Haydecker, you've gone too far this time! Murder?" Mad Harold's high spirits were returning.

"Me, murder? You've probably been lurking around these halls all night preying on unsuspecting women." Haydecker dropped the kidding. "Don't you really know her, Simpson?"

Haydecker thought it was only fair to call Mad Harold by his last name as a return favor. She had never quite had the courage to call him Mad Harold to his face. Just she and Ozzie did.

"She sure isn't a regular in this building, either as a tenant or as a visitor. Some of the folks have some pretty regular visitors, but she isn't one of them."

"Look!" Harold and Haydecker watched the scene in the foyer. The elevator door had opened once again releasing a photographer and some men in white uniforms carrying a gurney. Chubb and Sam were searching the floor of the foyer and hallway. Silent Sam disappeared down the long arm of the L that was out of the range of Wally's camera.

"Stop!" The command came booming from the TV sound box as a hurtling body appeared in view of the camera. Sam was in pursuit. Ozzie was awake and had come to get his own private viewing of the action. Sam grabbed him in a flash and, tucking the slight boy under his arm, prepared to carry him, all some 60 odd pounds of him, down the hall to 7F. Ozzie's last act for the moment was to stick out his tongue at Haydecker's camera.

Mad Harold and Haydecker laughed at seeing Ozzie hauled away. Harold added, "They don't know how many times they'll have to haul him off before they are through."

"So, what do you know, Harold?"

"Just about as much as you do. I had better get back out in the foyer for my grilling."

"Let me know anything you hear, huh?" Haydecker asked.

"Only if you'll keep an eye on the proceedings from up here. You really have a good view of the action. Let's keep each other posted."

"You can count on it, although you are still my No. 1 suspect. You just wanted some firsthand experience in criminal law, that's all. All the really great lawyers have to understand the criminal mind."

With a wave, Harold was gone. Mad Harold worked a split shift as The Towers doorman. He came on early from 6:30 to 9:00 to take care of the early morning rush, tore off for classes at University Law School and then returned for the evening shift from 5:00 until 10:30. At the end of the evening he walked the Haydecker's dog once again. Haydecker often wondered when he studied, or even if he studied. Even when he wasn't working, Harold always had time for a chat and sometimes, when a free lunch was offered, he would come back from classes at noon to keep Haydecker company. Her mother always saw to it that there was plenty extra in case a starving law student came around.

The front door buzzer sounded from Wally.

"Hey, Haydecker, let me in!" Ozzie was loose again. Haydecker punched the release button and Ozzie came storming into the bedroom.

"Hello, Ozzietwo."

"Haydecker, don't you dare "two" me. I can't help it if my name is the same as my dad's. I'll bet you didn't get to see the body."

"Wrong, Oz! I was out there within three feet of it."

Ozzie was crestfallen.

"I'll bet if you had left that dumb thing on all night you could have seen it happen." Ozzie gazed enviously at Wally and the TV screen.

"They don't usually inform me when a murder is going to happen on the seventh floor. Here is my homework for today. And, Ozzie, try not to drool all over it on the way to school."

"Shut up, Haydecker." He grabbed the papers and stomped out.

Haydecker knew from experience that a nasty insult was a good way to get rid of Ozzie--an insult to Ozzie usually was being reminded that he was the youngest kid.

Haydecker glanced at the monitor. Chubb and Sam were still searching the hall. A white outline now marked the place where Miss Plaid Lump had lain. Her body was gone and with it the men in the white coats and the photographers. Everything was almost the same but not quite the same as before.

"Breakfast!" Mrs. Haydecker appeared in the doorway with a tray. Haydecker was drawn away from the TV.

"Emily," her mother began as she settled on the side of the bed. Haydecker eyed the oatmeal suspiciously.

"I want you to listen very carefully, Emily. I have spoken to the detectives and they have agreed to let me go to work today after I have been interviewed. They are also coming in to interview you. I won't leave until they are finished, but we are short-staffed at the hospital and I may have to take over in an IC Unit. My nurses aren't supposed to get sick but we can't have them sniffling around in an Intensive Care Unit with the flu."

Haydecker was still looking at the oatmeal as though it had oozed out from under a rock. Why couldn't she have cocoa-puffs or fruit loops?

"Who was she, Mom?"

"Emily, you haven't heard a word I have been saying!"

"Oh, yes, I have. Your nurses have the flu and you have to go in to work today. Do you know who the girl was?" Emily wouldn't be put off.

"No one I have ever seen. Nor do I understand why it happened on our floor--this is a respectable apartment building. Murders don't happen here." Mrs. Haydecker shivered and hugged her white sweater closer to her white uniform. "At any rate, Haydecker. . . Emily, I don't want you to let anyone--that means anyone--in today."

"What about Woof?"

"I'll try to get off during my lunch hour for a quick stop at home-- otherwise I will have to make other arrangements, but I will let you know."

"Are you afraid?"

"The detectives said that they will post a policeman in the building when Harold is not on duty. Sure, I am a little afraid. Let's hope they get to the bottom of it quickly."

Chapter III

The door buzzer rang. Chubb and Silent Sam, unaware that they were on television, stood at the door, their faces distorted from being too close to the camera. The distortion certainly didn't improve things.

Haydecker punched Wally's door button and said, "Come on in." The knob being turned was picked up by the sound system. Chubb tried the door, opened it, and disappeared from view, followed by Sam. Mrs. Haydecker went out into the living room to meet them. Woof followed her as silently as Sam had followed Chubb.

Coming back, Woof gracefully leaped up on the end of Haydecker's bed, arranged himself to best advantage and stared at the detectives as if daring them to question his right to be on the bed. Mrs. Haydecker brought chairs to the bedside for the two men and then again settled on the end of the bed beside Woof. He snuggled close to her.

"Mrs. Haydecker," it was Chubb, "I am Captain Whitman and this is Detective Maker." Haydecker thought to herself that "Chubb" and "Silent Sam" fit better.

"We just need to ask a few questions so you can get on to work. We'll start with you since, as Head of Nursing at Wellington General, you are considered essential personnel. Our best guess is that the victim died about mid-night last night. Can you account for your whereabouts last evening?"

"About 6:30 last night Mr. Haydecker and I left here for the airport where he was taking a 9:20 flight to Dallas on a business trip."

"What airline?"

"United."

"You arrived back here at what time?"

"I didn't wait at the airport for take-off so I guess that I must have been here about ten after eight or so. The garage attendant should remember, he logs us in and out. I took the elevator straight up from the garage to the seventh floor."

"Did you see anything suspicious?"

"I saw nobody but the garage attendant. I did have trouble getting the elevator to stop at this floor."

"What do you mean?"

"When I punched the seventh floor, it zoomed right past to ten, but when the door opened on ten, nobody was there. So I punched seven again." Mrs. Haydecker explained slowly, trying to recall the events of the past night.

"Did it work that time?"

"As a matter of fact, now that I think of it, it didn't work that time either. I went down to six. I was so disgusted, I got off and walked up the one flight. I mean to report it to Mr. Bonomolo this morning."

Silent Sam was carefully recording the notes of the conversation.

"What about the rest of the evening?"

"I settled Emily down and tucked her in at the usual time of 9:30." Haydecker made a face. It had been years since her mother had tucked her in--a good night, yes, but a tuck-in--definitely not!

"At about 10:35 or 40, Harold Simpson, the doorman, came up to take Woof for a walk around the block. Mr. Haydecker doesn't like for me to have to go out at that hour of the night so Harold came as always and brought Woof back around 11:00." She scratched Woof behind the ears. He responded with a "hummm" at the back of his throat. "Neither time Harold was at the door did I see anyone in the foyer. I can assure you that the dead person was definitely not there at 11:00."

"Where does Harold Simpson go from here?" Chubb inquired. "Home, I suppose. He is finished at the Towers until the next morning." She shrugged.

Chubb addressed Sam, "Remember to ask Harold Simpson if he noted any elevator trouble in the last day or two."

Mrs. Haydecker continued, "I went to bed about 11:15 after securing the apartment and checking to see that Wally here was off."

"Wally, who is Wally?" Sam finally spoke in a low, croaking voice.

"Wally is this monitor and console of Emily's--sort of like an electronic babysitter and nurse. Her father built it when she made it clear that she was too old for a babysitter and not ill enough for a full time nurse." Mrs. Haydecker smiled wryly, "I am sure that Emily can answer any questions about Wally that you will need to know."

"Thank you. Mrs. Haydecker, that will be all for now unless you think of something else. We will ask Emily here a few questions and then make our rounds of the other tenants. We will probably get back to you. Don't worry, we will be keeping an eye on things around here. However, take no unnecessary risks until we understand what has been happening."

Mrs. Haydecker gave Woof a last ruffle and kissed Haydecker on the cheek, "I'll check in with you, sweetheart, and your father should call sometime this morning. Be sure to break the news of this event gently. Otherwise he will want to fly home right away." Haydecker was comforted by the idea that he would be here in a flash is they asked.

A few moments later the front door closed and the two detectives stared at the retreating back of Mrs. Haydecker as she headed toward the elevator. Waiting for it to stop at the floor, she glanced over at the camera and blew Haydecker a kiss. The detectives looked away embarrassed as if it were meant for them. Haydecker was used to the parting ritual. She wondered if Chubb and Sam had families of their own.

"Well, young lady," Chubb started the interview still staring at the monitor, long after Mrs. Haydecker had disappeared behind the elevator doors.

Chubb cleared his throat and started again, "Well, young lady," the digital numbers on Wally's console blinked an exact 8:30, "now, explain this contraption to me." It was plain to see that Chubb and Sam were, at the moment, more interested in Wally than in Miss Plaid Lump's murder.

Haydecker sighed with resignation and launched into an explanation. "My father, who is an electronic engineer, built Wally as a kind of all-purpose servant which can be operated entirely from my bed here as I am supposed to be in bed most of the time. Wally can work with the TV cameras in the foyer so I can see who is at the door." Haydecker worked the buttons to show them.

"So you can see out into the foyer all the time?"

"If I want to--but I don't usually spend the day watching what's not happening in the empty foyer."

Chubb looked thoughtful. Sam didn't say anything.

"Do you want me to finish?" Haydecker tried to keep the question from sound too sassy, although she was a little disgusted.

"By all means, what else does Wally do?"

"Wally opens and closes the drapes," Haydecker responded by demonstrating, "operates 130TV channels including channel 14 which is hooked up to my classroom at Pelham School every morning from 9:00 to 11:30. I can attend my classes and even answer questions from my teacher. They can't see me but, if Miss Gregg pushes the right button, she can hear my answers. Sometimes she has trouble remembering which is the right button to push."

"Do you mean you go to school right here in bed? What about the homework?"

"Ozzie, the kid you met out in the hall, Ozzie, he delivers it and brings things home for me."

Chubb and Sam were quite amazed by Wally. Haydecker simply had come to take him for granted.
"Can't you ever go to school or go out to play?"

"No. I don't usually have any difficulty with the class work...but two afternoons a week somebody called an itinerant teacher comes to help me with the work, a Mr. Plimpton. We usually talk about other stuff. Even though he got fired from the public schools, Mr. Plimpton knows a lot about a lot of things. We don't talk about school work much."

"Why did Mr. Plimpton get fired?" Mr. Chubb was curious about everything. Haydecker was beginning to think he wasn't such a dope after all.

"Mostly, I think, because he came to school smelling like Jim Beam or, at least, that's what some of the other kids said."

Chubb looked a little surprised. "What do you know about Jim Beam, young lady?"

"Well," Haydecker was a little miffed that he thought she was that young and dumb, "I can tell by the smell when Plimp comes into the room."

"I take it that 'Plimp' is this teacher. Why in the world would they hire him?"

"Because they can't get anyone else for that little pay and for work that is not regular, I suppose. He is qualified, you know, and he is perfectly nice and he is always pretty sober when he comes here. Otherwise my parents wouldn't let him come."

"When was the last time that Mr. Plimpton was here?"

"He comes on Tuesdays and Thursdays."

Chubb seemed satisfied on the subject of Mr. Plimpton.

Haydecker went on to describe the further wonders of Wally, "There is also a built in phone system and a special intercom to the front door of the building to that I can talk to Mad Harold."

"Mad Harold?"

"Harold Simpson. He is the doorman who walks Woof."

Woof stirred uneasily at the end of the bed. He wished those strange men would leave. His whole morning routine was definitely upset.

"Just what do you know about this Simpson?"

"Oh, he goes to law school and works at this building. He's a real brain and doesn't have to study much. When I have trouble with my math, he is the one I can ask. Besides, he is around a lot. It's like having my own special math tutor rather than having to wait in class to have a question answered. He also teaches me extra things that the other kids won't learn until Advanced Algebra."

"Bleep!" A red light appeared on Wally's console.

Haydecker, enjoying showing Wally off, punched a button and said, "Hello, Haydecker here."

"Hello, Scarecrow, what's new?" Haydecker usually didn't mind the nickname from her father, but she would rather he hadn't used it in front of the detectives. And she had asked him especially not to use it when Ozzie was around. That's all she needed was for Ozzie to get a hold of that nickname. He would spread in all over Pelham. Then she would really have to punch out some of his permanent teeth.

"Oh, hi, Dad, lots of excitement here this morning. There was a dead body in front of the elevator when we woke up this morning."

"What? Emily be serious." There was a pause. "Where is your mother?"

Before Haydecker could answer, Chubb had signaled that he wanted to talk.

"Mr. Haydecker, this is Lieutenant Whitman of the detective squad speaking. Mrs. Haydecker is just fine and has gone to the hospital. We, my partner, Detective Maker, and I are interviewing Emily as a matter of procedure.

"Who was the dead person? Anyone we know?" The voice over the wire sounded a little relieved.

"The body has not yet been identified nor has the cause of death been determined. As far as we know at this time, it was no one known by any of the residents of this floor. We are posting a guard in the building for a few days. Just until we know more about the situation."

"Thank you, Lieutenant. Emily, do you want me to come home today? I can leave on the next flight out."

"It is not necessary, Dad. Things are calmer and I have Wally and Woof and Harold if I need anything. Mom only went to the hospital because there was an emergency.

"OK, stay in bed, Scarecrow, and I will call again. How is your mother holding up?"

"Oh, you know Mom. She's at her best in a crisis!"

"I'll talk to you tonight."

"Bye, Dad."

"Will he call every day?" It was Silent Sam, alias Detective Maker, who asked the question.

"Mostly, when he can."

"So, what else can Wally do?" Chubb, alias Whitman, was back in his question-asking form.

"He can control the drapes. I can load my IPod and it hooks to my cell phone. I guess I told you that. He controls the heat in the apartment by room and can turn on the oven or the microwave. He can do practically everything except brush my teeth. I have to do that for myself. He's also got a computer with a built in word-processing program so that if I want to do my homework that way, I can. Someday, and I hope I am not still here, I will be able to send my homework to school through the computer. Then I won't need Ozzie except to bring home papers."

"Some set up! Do you like not going to school? It must be great not having to get up every morning." Obviously, Chubb had not liked school very much.

Haydecker gave him a thoughtful look. "I still have to do all the school work without having any of the fun of being with my friends. School isn't so bad you know. I am here alone most days." Haydecker thought if they only knew how long the days got.

"How come you don't have a nurse or a babysitter?"

Haydecker sniffed and looked away. "We tried that! I am not sick enough for a nurse and too old for those darn baby sitters who wanted to fuss at me all the time. I am nearly thirteen and perfectly capable of taking care of myself."

"I would think your parents would be worried about your staying in bed."

"That was part of the deal. If I could stay alone and not have one of those sitters, I would behave myself. I want to get well as soon as possible so I can get back to the real world. This is enough of the twilight zone. It really isn't any fun, you know!"

Haydecker decided to spare the detective the details of how she managed to get rid of Nurse Buns (nickname for Myrtle Bernstein) and Gorgon Grace (alias for Grace Stern, the sitter). She wasn't all that sorry that they had both left. It had taken a lot of maneuvering. Thank goodness her father had understood and created Wally. It had taken a lot more persuasion to bring her mother around.

The red light blinked on the top of the TV screen.

"I'm sorry, but my school is about to start. That light means my teacher is signaling, that she is turning on the system. You are welcome to stay."

Haydecker tried not to make it sound too friendly.

"No, we will come back at another time to find out what else you may know about this business. By the way, Miss Haydecker. . ." Chubb cleared his throat.

Haydecker raised her mental eyebrows. First it was "young lady"; then it was "Emily"; and now it was "Miss Haydecker". She was a little wary.

Haydecker flicked on the picture to reveal Miss Gregg writing on the blackboard. She left the sound off--nothing was happening yet.

"Miss Haydecker, I wouldn't want you to miss school or anything like that but I was wondering if you might like to assist this investigation by keeping any eye on the foyer whenever you can. Who knows, you might spot something or someone useful to our inquiry. You understand, this is unofficial and off the record, of course." He ran his finger under his collar as if it had suddenly become too tight. Of course, it was, a little.

Haydecker grinned. She understood perfectly. They would be in trouble for asking, if anyone found out. She knew her mother would be furious.

"I was intending to do just that. It can be useful to know what everyone is doing. It isn't like I have much else to do, is it?" Haydecker answered.

Chubb grinned back. They understood each other.

"We will come back for another conversation later. Have a good day, Miss Haydecker. And, if you notice anything suspicious, call us immediately. Take no action yourself. Rest assured that we will keep our men in the building at all times so that you needn't worry about your safety." Chubb put on his grimmest face.

"I understand. See you later."

The detectives disappeared into the silent living room and Haydecker heard the door close. She flipped to the door camera to see the stiff backs of Chubb and Sam going across the foyer. They knew they were being watched.

Haydecker pushed the lock button for the front door and switched the TV set in time to hear Miss Gregg say, "Emily, Emily, are you there? It is class time."

"I'm here, Miss Gregg. I'm sorry I'm late. We have just had an interesting morning in our apartment building." Haydecker waited until she was sure that the whole classroom was listening to their exchange. "About dawn a murdered girl was found in front of the seventh floor elevator."

The class erupted. There was a babble of questions. Emily Marie Haydecker smiled to herself and to Woof who was sleeping soundly, unaware that the 8th grade at Pelham Middle School had just heard a block-buster piece of news.

It would be a few minutes before Miss Gregg would be able to start class. Meanwhile, Haydecker had the floor to herself. This was almost as good as being there, almost. She was looking forward to giving them further updates.

She had a ring-side seat for what would happen next.

Chapter IV

Emily Marie Haydecker attended school from her bed that Monday morning as she did every Monday morning, and Tuesday, and Wednesday, and so on. She would have been the first to admit that very little of her mind was on the math problems. She could already add, subtract, multiply and divide decimals and understood the basics of algebra.

She knew she could do the problems for the week because she had already finished them. She had had a little help from Mad Harold. Her mind was on things more interesting than decimals. What's more, it took her mind off of her aching legs and arms.

Haydecker, propped up on her pillows in bed with her controls, flipped back and forth from her classroom at school to the 7th floor foyer of the Towers. She tried to time things so that Miss Gregg would not be able to detect her absence from the classroom. It was tricky because Haydecker was pretty sure that there was a faint click on the speaker system when she switched. But so far, Miss Gregg had been too busy to catch her. That is what she thought, but she didn't know. She needed to be careful that she didn't get caught and ruin the whole set up.

The morning dragged. The foyer was empty. The class, after listening to Haydecker's description of the early morning scene on the 7th floor of Hatterfield Towers, wasn't attending much to decimals or gerunds. Nor were they even moved in reading class by the tale of Ajax or Achilles or some such Greek person being dragged around by the heel in the Trojan War.

The front door buzzer rang. Haydecker flipped to the camera at the front door. Mrs. Golda Heifitz stood there smiling self-consciously at the camera. She was holding Ramona under her arm. Ramona was just one of Mrs. Heifitz's cats. When Mrs. Heifitz visited, one, and only one, of the cats was permitted to visit along with her. One cat at a time was all that Woof could bear on his turf. And then, it was just scarcely bearable. The cats were, in order of visitation rights: Morton, Samuel, Rachel, Ramona, and Caesar.

"Come in, Mrs. Heifitz." Haydecker scanned the hall. No one else. She pushed the door release. Woof lifted his head and stirred restlessly, rearranging his chin on his paws. He recognized the name.

After a pause, not of the feline kind, Mrs. Heifitz entered the bedroom. Woof's neck hairs rose even when his body remained still. He knew he must be a gentleman and behave himself. But that didn't make him like cats.

"Hello, Dearie, I thought you might be able to use a bit of company. Your morning school is about done, isn't it?" Haydecker knew that Mrs. Heifitz didn't have the slightest idea when the school was done; she obviously wanted to talk to someone and, as was usual in the morning, Haydecker was one of the few residents left on the 7th floor of the Towers. She kind of liked Mrs. Heifitz.

"I just came up from downstairs talking to Mr. Bonomolo. I thought you might like to know the news." Haydecker lay back on her pillows and kept the monitor trained on the hall. The class was doing tomorrow's math.

"What did Tony have to say about the murder?" For once, Haydecker was as curious as Mrs. Heifitz. A person had to go some to be as curious as Mrs. Heifitz.

"Well, . . ." Golda Heifitz launched into her tale. "You can imagine how excited he is--talking as if he is fit to be tied--hardly a moment for stopping to take a breath. No one seems to know the girl, at least, no one will admit to knowing her, yet. Mr. Bonomolo is afraid the apartment owners will fire him because a murder took place in the building he manages.

"Does he have an alibi?"

"An alibi--dearie, what's that. I don't know as I even have one of those."

Haydecker broke it down for her as it was obvious Mrs. Heifitz did not watch much TV, at least not much but soaps. "It means can he prove where he was at the time of the murder."

"Oh, dear me, he's not afraid they will fire him because they think he did it. He's just thinking that he doesn't run a very respectable building," Mrs. Heifitz sat further forward on the edge of her seat.

She went on, "According to Tony, it seems like they are having some trouble deciding just where and when she died. But Tony says he was in his apartment all evening except for making some rounds about eight o'clock."

"It seems that Tony would hardly have killed her and dumped the body in the foyer. What is your alibi, Mrs. Heifitz? Have the police detectives questioned you yet?"

"Oh, my, yes, dearie. I was in my apartment all evening with the kittens, who can't very well vouch for me, can they? I did talk on the telephone some during the evening."

Haydecker smiled to herself. Mrs. Heifitz was notorious for her many and long phone conversations with her six sisters all living in the city. They didn't get out much to get together, so they telephoned a lot.

"As for the rest of the hall, most everyone I've heard of seems to have, what do you call it, an 'abali'. Sara and Dee were out for dinner at a friend's house. The Browers were all at a concert at Maria's school and they attended a reception afterward. The McCaws were at home except for the Mr. being out on city business. It was a school night so Ozzie had to be in bed early. Mrs. McCaw, she doesn't go out much anyway. Let me see, now, what else."

"How did you find out all this about where everybody was?" Haydecker asked, knowing it was rude to ask, but she couldn't help it. Mrs. Heifitz, true to her name of Golda, was always a gold mine of information.

"Well, dearie, if you just stand around down stairs for a while, you can hear a lot. Oh, I remember, General Cargill came through the lobby about 8:30 and, for some strange reason which he didn't explain, took the stairs--can you imagine--instead of the elevator. A 68 year-old man with a war wound, taking the stairs seven floors. I'm surprised he didn't plop over himself!' Mrs. Heifitz's voice wandered off.

She didn't get on too well with the General. The General thought she was too nosy and wanted to be too friendly. Mrs. Heifitz disturbed the General's schedule. Haydecker had secretly thought that probably the General was afraid that Mrs. Heifitz was out to snag him. She couldn't imagine the General married to all the Heifitz cats.

"Anyway, Ramona and I came over to see about your lunch and see if you had any as I am fixing a little extra and could easily bring you over a tray? It isn't good for people to go without eating a little hot food at a meal, especially young people can't go around eating cold meals all the time. Too many snacks these days."

"Thanks, Mrs. Heifitz, but mom put something in the oven for me before she left; it is warming right now. You wouldn't have an extra onion roll or two, though, would you?" Golda Heifitz, several time a week, made the best onion rolls Haydecker at ever eaten.

Mrs. Heifitz smiled broadly, patting her tightly curled hair with her beringed fingers, "Well, now, I just happen to have some nice fresh ones. I will bring you over a couple to have with your lunch. I'll be back in a minute." Golda Heifitz whisked out of the bedroom and was at the front door almost before Haydecker could reach for the release button.

Haydecker mused that Golda Heifitz appreciated being appreciated. It didn't matter if it was a fresh onion roll or fresh news, Golda needed something to be appreciated for. But didn't everyone.

Haydecker glanced into the hall to follow Golda's back around the corner. Ramona's fluffy tail drooped from under Golda's plump arm.

The elevator light went on; Haydecker waited with interest to see who would get off. The doors opened; while the shadow caused by the overhead light in the elevator showed that someone was inside, no one emerged. Haydecker dismissed it as someone having punched the wrong floor. The doors closed again.

Haydecker was just about to look away when the doors opened again and a man, looking anxiously at Golda's door, or at least in that direction, stepped out of the elevator. He peered furtively from under the brim of a black hat pulled down over his forehead. He went immediately to the potted rubber plant that stood just beside the elevator door. Taking something from his pocket, he slipped it into one of the huge leaves of the plant. All the while, he was glancing up and looking toward Golda's apartment door. After seeming to deposit something in one of the leaves of the plant, he slipped quickly back onto the elevator and the doors closed him from view.

Haydecker sat up straight, itching to know what, if anything, he had put in the plant leaf. But she knew she would run into either Golda or her mother if she were to go into the foyer just now. She briefly wondered if she should call Chubb and Sam, only briefly.

Haydecker went to the kitchen where her lunch tray was laid out, except for getting the casserole from the oven. She quickly went back to watch the monitor in the bedroom.

Golda appeared around the corner without the cat and moving more slowly because she was carrying a plate covered with a linen napkin. As she was approaching the door, smiling to herself, behind her, the elevator door opened and again out stepped the same man in the black coat, his dark hat pulled down over his eyes as before.

Golda glanced at him and sprinted to Haydecker's door and whispered loudly, "Emily, please let me in!"

Haydecker pushed the button. "It's open."

Golda disappeared from view.

The black-coated man darted to the plant and seemed to retrieve what he had put there before. "Or did he," Haydecker wondered. Had she missed something while she was in the kitchen? Had he taken something from the same one of the huge leaves or had he hidden it.

"Oh, Emily Marie," Golda Heifitz was breathless from the excitement, "did you see that strange man? I wonder what he wanted. Did you see where he went?" The words tumbled all over each other as the onion rolls slid onto the carpet. Golda flapped into a chair fanning herself with the napkin.

Haydecker decided she wouldn't get Mrs. Heifitz excited any further, especially as there wasn't apt to be anything in the plant when she finally looked. To tell Golda would probably overexcite her.

"I don't know what he wanted. He just got back on the elevator." That part was true. He had come and gone as quickly the second time as he had the first. Emily realized suddenly with a jolt that probably he had not yet seen the camera above the door and didn't know he had been observed.

"I'll be glad when the get this murder business cleared up," Golda remarked, breathing a little easier. "It seems we'll all be afraid of our own shadows." Haydecker hadn't been afraid until Golda started talking about it.

The door buzzer rang. Haydecker looked up to see her mother standing in the hall with her arms full of packages. "Can you unlock the door, Emily? I have my hands full." Mrs. Haydecker hadn't been able to reach her handbag to find her key.

She was soon in the bedroom dropping her parcels in the empty chair. Removing her gloves, she said, "I just passed the rudest man in the downstairs foyer. He charged off the elevator and nearly knocked me over."

"Was he dressed in a long, dark overcoat and a dark hat pulled down over his eyes?" Haydecker asked.

"Exactly, how did you know?" Mrs. Haydecker looked up, surprised.

"Because he was just up here in the hall." Haydecker answered.

"He nearly scared me out of my wits, coming up behind me," Mrs. Heifitz huffed. "It seems that a person can't be safe in their own home these days." Golda was breathing hard again.

Mrs. Haydecker tried to soothe the older woman. "I think he is long gone by now. But can I get you a cup of tea, Golda, to calm your nerves?"

"No, no, if you're sure he's gone, I must get back to my little family. It is time for Kitty Bits."

"Thanks for the onion rolls, Mrs. Heifitz." Haydecker was chewing on one while talking. Mrs. Haydecker give a frown and a shake of her head.

"Yes, thanks, Golda. You are so good to Emily Marie," the voices of the two women faded as they walked out of the bedroom and toward the front door.

"I'll stay here at the door until you get around the corner," Mrs. Haydecker promised, her voice loud again once the door was opened and the microphone picked up the conversation.

Golda scurried out of sight and Mrs. Haydecker waited a few moments until she heard a door close down the hall. Haydecker was itching to check the plant but for the life of her could not think of any good excuses for her mother letting her go out in the foyer. She was stuck in the apartment until her mother went back to work.

The phone buzzed.

"Haydecker residence. Emily speaking." Haydecker thought she had better get polite and answer the telephone right since it was during business hours and the call might be for her mother or father, especially from one of her father's offices.

Mrs. Haydecker answered, too, and took the call since it was from the hospital reporting that the ICU was fully staffed for the afternoon. Haydecker groaned. Her mother wouldn't be returning to work.

Mrs. Haydecker finished the phone call and buzzed on the intercom from the kitchen, "Emily, when you've finished your lunch, snuggle down and take a nap and turn Wally off for a couple of hours. We were up awfully early this morning."

"Oh, Mother, you know I'm not sleepy and I am too old to be napping."

"Emily, do you want to get well or don't you? Do it right now!"

Haydecker had no intention of actually closing her eyes but. . .staring at the empty hall on the TV monitor was dull and she soon drifted off to sleep leaving Wally to persistently but mindlessly stare at the expanse of carpet in the foyer.

The next thing Haydecker knew, she awoke to the buzzing of the doorbell. The monitor had been turned off and the drapes closed while she slept. She was disgusted with herself. Every time she made an argument to her mother about not being sleepy, she managed, with little trouble, to fall asleep. No wonder her mother didn't pay attention to her. This growing up was tough.

The doorbell buzzed again and Haydecker flipped on Wally just in time to hear her mother opening the door to Ozzietwo.

"I'm sorry, Ozzie, but Emily is asleep right now and can't see you. Can you come back later?"

"No, I'm not, Mom." Haydecker cut in. Ordinarily she wasn't so keen on seeing Ozzietwo but today she had plans for him. "Let him come in with my homework. I am anxious to get started on it." Haydecker blushed at the little at the lie.

Ozzietwo darted under Mrs. Haydecker's arm and dashed for the bedroom before his friend's mother could veto the plan.

"Hi, Oz, how's it going?"

Ozzietwo stopped short, getting suspicious. Haydecker usually greeted him with some insult and she always called him Ozzietwo just to make him mad.

Woof got up, sniffed and stretched. He liked Ozzietwo and usually encouraged a wrestling match in the afternoons when Ozzietwo came home from school. Ozzie, ignoring Woof, was still waiting warily to see what had prompted the change in Haydecker's behavior.

Haydecker waited a moment to see if her mother was going to come into the room. She beckoned Ozzietwo to come closer. He came near the bed slowly, still not trusting his frienemy.
"Hey, Oz, there is something I want you to do."

"What?" Ozzietwo didn't give anything away. "Maybe I will and maybe I won't."

"Oh, come on, Oz, this isn't a trick of any kind. This morning a man in a black coat and hat got off the elevator and put something in the big plant by the elevator door. Go search the leaves of the plant and see if you can find anything. Quick! The General is just coming out into the foyer."

Ozzietwo jet-propelled through the living room and out the Haydecker front door. The General stopped abruptly and looked at Ozzietwo who had also stopped just as suddenly. The two eyed each other.

"Well, young man, what do you think you're doing skipping school this afternoon? It's bad enough that we have one truant child in this building. What is this generation of children going to come to!"

"But, Mr. . . .I mean, General Cargill," Haydecker could tell that Ozzietwo was thinking fast, "school is over for the day. I just got home. Besides sir, Haydecker, I mean, Emily Marie, is really sick with rheumatic fever and can't go to school. I get to help her out."

"Good old Ozzie!" Haydecker thought. While they didn't usually get along, she could count on him in a pinch. What business was it of the General's whether she went to school or not?

Ozzietwo stood his ground outside the door of the apartment with his back to the camera. Haydecker could just imagine the innocent, idiot grin on his face, looking like he had never done anything wrong in his whole life. She had to hand it to Ozzietwo. He could really act. He was Golden Globe material.

The General looked confused for a moment and then went, "Hump humph," and, giving Ozzietwo a piercing stare, returned the way he had come, muttering about taking these young people in hand. Haydecker heard his apartment door, out of camera view, slam. Apparently he had forgotten why he had come out into the hall.

Ozzietwo turned around, giving an all-teeth grin at the camera and, he hoped, Haydecker. He raised his hands above his head, his fists clenched. Then he turned around and tore over to the rubber plant.

Ozzietwo could move. Haydecker figured he'd be another Carl Lewis someday. He had already won intermediate relays at Pelham last spring. It was really something for a fourth grader to win against the fifth and sixth grade runners in the spring events.

Oz2 dug into the plant's leaves with vengeance, his eyes darting down the hall and then back to the plant. He picked something out of the second leaf and quickly stuffed it into his behind blue jeans pocket. It was a little bit of a tight struggle as they were last year's jeans.

He had just extracted his hand from his pocket when the elevator bell chimed and the light went on above the door.

Ozzietwo dropped down on one knee.

"What's he doing now," Haydecker stormed to herself, anxious to see what he had found.

The elevator opened and Chubb and Sam stepped off, "Well, youngster, what are you doing here?" It was a surprising Silent Sam who asked the question.

 "Just tying my shoe, Detective. I suppose you've found the murderer already?" Even to Haydecker, it sounded it a little 'smart-mouth'.

"Just never you mind, young man, just leave the detection to us and stay out of these halls. It is no place to be loitering around. If I see you again, I will have to report you to your parents.

"But, Detective, I was just fixing my shoe, besides, I don't even know what loitering is. So how can I be doing it?"

"Well, from now on, get dressed at home, do you hear? Now get along to your apartment." Ozzietwo had no choice but to head off out of camera range down the hall toward 7F. Haydecker groaned. Ozzietwo had the evidence and just disappeared down the hall. At least, she hoped it was some evidence. What this case needed was some evidence.

Chubb and Sam proceeded to search the foyer once again. This time they were both down on their hands and knees dragging their hands across the surface of the carpet. They started in the center of the foyer and worked outward from the spot where Miss Plaid Lump had lain.

The phone buzzed. She punched Wally's button.

"Hey, Haydecker? Ozzie. I got something. Ozzietwo's voice really squeaked. He must have something important. He never squeaked that high.

"The fuzz is still in the hall so you will have to wait a few minutes. I will call you when they are gone. It is better not to tempt the fates or they might frisk you."

"Frisk me, oh, Haydecker. Get serious! If they would tell my dad, I'd be grounded for 10 million years. You would probably have to start bring my homework to me. Don't call. My mom isn't feeling too hot. I'll call you again in a few minutes to see if the coast is clear."

Ozzietwo's mother was never too well and scarcely ever left her apartment. Ozzieone, her husband, Ozzie's dad, worked downtown at city hall and was really active in political stuff. Haydecker had often seen him on the evening TV news but had never really paid much attention to what was being talked about or what his position was. Ozzietwo didn't talk much about either one of his parents. They were just there.

Haydecker winced a little as it suddenly occurred to her that Ozzietwo must spend an awful lot of time alone, with his father gone so much and his mother doing what he called "resting" in her bedroom. No wonder the little brat was such a nuisance--coming around all the time. He probably didn't have anyone else to bug. Haydecker knew she should be more patient with him but it was hard when he pestered all the time. She would work on that.

Almost with a sixth sense, the telephone buzzed as Chubb and Sam got on the elevator. Haydecker pushed Wally's button. "Yep."

One of these days she was going to answer the phone like that thinking it was one of her friends and it would really be somebody. She had to be more careful.

"OK, yet, Haydecker?"

"The coast is just clear, Oz. Get down here but keep a careful look-out. You never know when those two will show up again. They might just have forgotten something.

Haydecker counted under her breath and, at the count of seven, Ozzietwo sped around the corner. That was a little slow for him, unless, of course, he had to tip-toe out of the apartment. Quiet always took longer.

Once on a rainy Saturday afternoon, Ozzie and Haydecker had practiced timing Oz2 from his door to hers. Haydecker remembered that as being an awful boring afternoon.

He presented himself before the camera, his face agrin with excitement, "Let me in, Haydecker." He stuck out his tongue.

"It's open." He was inside the bedroom in a flash, his hand pawing at the too-tight pocket on the rear of his jeans. Haydecker held her breath in case it split the zipper. Ozzietwo seemed to have lots of zipper trouble, anyway. He couldn't seem to remember to zip.

"Look, Haydecker." He opened his palm and revealed a key with a small slip of paper crudely attached with some ordinary plastic tape. The paper said "2300-1-28."

"Whaddaya think the key is to?" Ozzietwo was breathing extra hard. Haydecker supposed it was the excitement more than it was the exercise.

"It looks like an ordinary door key to me, "she answered. I'll get my apartment key and see if they are alike. Have you got yours with you?"

Haydecker bounced out of bed and rummaged around in her bureau drawer. It had been a long time since she had needed her apartment key to get in after coming home from school.

Ozzietwo merely reached down the neck of his sweatshirt and hauled his out at the end of a leather shoelace where he kept it handy so he wouldn't have to rouse his mother to get in and out of their apartment.

The three keys lay side-by-side on the bed comforter. They seemed alike, at least, they were the same in color and material but the grooves and bumps of the key codes did not match exactly.

Ozzietwo and Haydecker stared at one another. They each had a lot of unspoken questions.

Finally, Ozzietwo whispered, "Do you suppose this has anything to do with the murder?"

They were silent again for a long minute.

"It might," Haydecker answered still staring at the short row of keys. "I suppose we should tell Chubb and Sam." She didn't sound too definite.

Ozzietwo's face fell. "Who are Chubb and Sam and why should be tell them? If we tell anyone, we should tell the detectives."

Haydecker grinned at Ozzietwo, "They are the detectives, dopey, at least, that is what I call them. The tall, thin one is Silent Sam because he doesn't say much. The other one is Chubb, for the obvious reason. That is, however, Chubb with two "b's" to make him more important."

"Haydecker, you're crazy. You're always giving everyone nicknames. One of these days, I'm going to find a real winner for you. You'll hate it! You can count on it!"

"Relax, Oswald." That is what Haydecker lived in fear of, that he would find out that her father's pet name for her was "Scarecrow."

"Emily Marie Haydecker, lay off that Oswald stuff, too. It's bad enough being called 'nigger' and 'black boy' at school without you using my real name at home." Ozzietwo was trembling as he turned away to look out the window.

"When I get grown up, I am going to change my name to something ordinary like George Jones."

"I'll tell you what, Oz, let's pick detective code names since it looks like we've got a case here. Do you want to be Sherlock or Watson, or Charlie, after Charlie Chan?" Haydecker was pretty quickly trying to pour some oil on the troubled waters of Ozzietwo's feelings.

Ozzietwo turned back from the window, brightening at the idea of becoming a detective. "I sure don't want to be Sherlock--that is as bad as Oswald. I'll be Watson. Who are you going to be?"

"I'll be Hercule."

Watson had a laughing fit on the spot. He threw himself at the end of the bed. "What kind of a name is 'Airkool'?" The thought of it broke him up again. He banged his head against the mattress.

Haydecker was a little miffed. "For your information, Hercule Poirot is a famous detective in the mystery books of Agatha Christie. Don't you remember that movie on TV, 'Murder on the something or other express train'?"

"You mean the fat guy with the big, long muchstash from some foreign country?" The thought of it nearly broke Ozzietwo up all over again. He nearly kicked Woof with his Nike's.

"Belgium. He was from Belgium." Haydecker informed him of the fact with all the dignity she could muster. Ozzietwo was enjoying himself hugely. Haydecker wasn't.

Haydecker scowled, "All right, Watson. Let's get to work on these keys."

Ozzietwo got serious again. "Do we have to tell the detectives yet?"

"Maybe not yet." Haydecker was thinking hard. "They are going to be plenty mad that we didn't tell them about the possibility of something being hidden in the plant in the first place. Especially since you snitched it right from under their noses."

"Well, you told me to do it, Airkool, so you are just as guilty as I am."

Haydecker smiled, looking directly into Ozzietwo's big, brown eyes. "Hey, Watson, you were great out there in the hall with both the General and the detectives. You'll make a great detective.

Ozzietwo gave a face-splitting grin at Haydecker's praise. He was feeling better.

"Maybe, Airkool, we should see if the key fits one of the apartment doors on this floor," Watson suggested.

"Maybe, you're right, Watson. That shouldn't be too tough. The problem is, doing it without getting caught. Maybe late at night, for instance. Except that I think there are quite a lot of people in the halls around here at night. The people on this floor aren't exactly early-to-bedders and it would certainly look weird if a couple of kids were wandering around."

"We could try a couple disguises," Watson offered.

"Ozzietwo, no matter what disguises you put on, you are still going to look like a 4'5", 10 year-old black kid from the seventh floor and I would still look like 13 year-old, skinny, red-haired girl kid. At our sizes and ages, disguises aren't going to fool anyone"

Ozzietwo looked disappointed. "I guess we will just have to try the key on all the doors on this floor. If it doesn't work here, then we can go on to other floors."

"Yeah, but the thing to do is to start with the ones that won't get us charged with breaking and entering."

"What's breaking and entering when we have a key?"

"Haydecker answered, "It's still breaking and entering, I think, if we don't belong there."

"Well," Ozzietwo snapped back, "That leaves our apartment and your apartment and we won't find out much in either place."

"Oh, but my dear, Watson," Hercule reminded her faithful detective friend, "We have the Storage Room and we have 7A which is empty at the present moment and which wouldn't get us into too much trouble. Of course, there probably isn't anything in there anyway."

Ozzietwo's eyes lit up, "Excellent, my dear, Airkool, but how are we gonna do it without getting caught?"

The room was quiet. Woof's paws moved rhythmically in his sleep. Maybe he was chasing rabbits in a dream. But, how can you dream of rabbits if you have lived your whole life in a city apartment? Haydecker went back to thinking of a problem she could solve.

Mrs. Haydecker appeared in the doorway and moved over to punch Wally's console to close the drapes against the coming winter night, "Just what are you two plotting now?" It was a good thing she wasn't watching the faces of the two culprits when she asked the question. Oz2 and Haydecker looked at each other guiltily. Ozzietwo buried his face in Woof's neck to keep from giving it away.

"Will you be staying for dinner, Ozzie?" Mrs. Haydecker invited.

Ozzietwo's reply was a little muffled. "Thanks, Mrs. Haydecker, but I think my Mom is expecting me. She gets a little PO'd if she makes something and I am not there. If it is all right, I'll come back for dessert though." Ozzietwo was always good for an extra dessert. If he could get two desserts at dinner, he would.

Mrs. Haydecker said on her way out of the room, "Well, Emily, will be having her dinner in about 10 minutes so you might want to go home pretty soon."

"Thanks a lot, ma'am, but I don't have to go just yet. I got something I want to talk about with Emily yet." Mrs. Haydecker went on into the kitchen, humming tunelessly. Ozzietwo was notorious for not taking hints.

"Okay, Ozzie, I guess the only thing to do is to send you out as an advance man to do the detection because I am sure not going to get out of here tonight. Mom is home for the evening and that means I am stuck."

"Whaddaya mean, advance man? Haydecker, is that just a fancy way of saying that I have do it alone?"

"Oh, come on, Oz, you're tough. You can do it!"

"Yeah, and I can also get caught alone."

 "I'll help out, Oz, we can get your walkie-talkies and I will keep an eye on things from the monitor. It any one comes, I can warn you."

Watson, better known as Ozzietwo, grinned, and his eyes lit up. At last the Christmas gift of walkie-talkies would come in useful. He had tried and tried to get Haydecker to help him experiment with them but she had always brushed him off as being too childish. Now he would show her that they were not just a little kid's toy.

"I'll run and get them and we'll check the batteries. Let me out, Airkool." Ozzietwo was off and running out the front almost before Haydecker could get to the button. She watched him disappear around the corner and reappear almost immediately and present himself at the camera.

"Let me in, Haydecker, I forgot my key." He was a little embarrassed. He raced in and grabbed his key with the string attached and was off again.

Haydecker lay back in the pillows feeling tired from just being around Ozzietwo's speed and energy. There was a day when she could have kept up with him. If only she were well, too, and able to run. Although she realized that at her age, she would probably not do it if she were well. There was such a thing as dignity.

Ozzietwo, alias, Watson, didn't return immediately as she had expected and Mrs. Haydecker came into the room with her dinner tray. "What, is Ozzie gone? I thought he intended to stay, at least, for dessert. I brought an extra piece of cake. I figure it doesn't affect his appetite to eat his dessert before his main meal."

"Oh, he'll be back." Haydecker watched the monitor. It was a busy time in the hall. "He just went home to get a Christmas gift to show me." Haydecker thought she had better try sticking just as close to the truth as possible whenever she could.

"A Christmas gift? Isn't it a little past the holiday. Christmas has been over for a month. Enjoy your dinner. I'll come and join you in a few minutes. This has been such a hectic day that I don't really feel like eating."

"Oops, here he comes again." Haydecker talked with her mouth full as she punched the door button.

Ozzietwo breezed in with a walkie-talkie unit in each hand.

"Here's your cake, Watson. Eat it so you'll have a lot of energy for detecting." Haydecker teased knowing that no one would have to beg Oz2 to eat the ample wedge of cake Haydecker's mother had supplied.

He immediately stuffed in a mouthful and began to talk, "Of course, Mother wanted to know what I wanted the walkie-talkies for." He grabbed for Haydecker's glass of milk to wash down the huge mouthful of cake.

"What did you tell her?"

"Oh, I just mumbled something about trying them out. Something about how you hadn't seen them since Christmas." Ozzietwo polished off Haydecker's milk.

"Do you suppose they would work all the way to school, if we tried them?"

Haydecker thought it over. "Probably not. After all, Pelham is twelve blocks away. We can ask my Dad about it though. He knows pretty much about all that electronic stuff. Maybe if they wouldn't work how they are now, maybe he could fix them up."

"Yeah, I suppose so," went with another huge bite of the chocolate cake.

"Now, here is my plan." Haydecker started as soon as the cake no longer had Watson's full attention. "I have been keeping track of who has come home from work on the floor. We have only a few to go. My Mom is home. I am assuming the General and Mrs. Heifitz are both still in their apartments since I didn't see them go out this afternoon. Marcia Brower came home with her brother about 5:30 and Sara and DD came in just a few minutes ago. Miss Gerot came in loaded with papers right after school. That leaves only your dad and Miss Onken. My dad won't be coming tonight. He's out of town."

"My dad's usually pretty late, if he comes home for dinner at all. It didn't look like my mom was fixing for him since its gonna be 'mac and cheese' tonight and he hates mac and cheese.' I get it quite a lot. I don't mind as long as there is lots of it."

"Go out in the living room, Watson, and let's try these things out. How do they work?"

Watson explained the mechanical details to his partner. He flitted off to the living room in his soundless sneakers and, amid crackling, his voice came loudly through the black box when Haydecker pressed the right lever.

"Now, Haydecker, you have to say 'Roger' and 'Over and Out' and stuff like that."

"We don't have to do anything of the sort! All we have to do is get you in and out of the Storage Room without been seen." Haydecker

---

was getting a little nervous and also feeling a little guilty about forcing Ozzietwo to go it alone.

"Okay, Watson, have you got the key?"

"Roger," Ozzietwo would do it his way.

"The front door is open. I'll just leave it unlocked. You go quickly and see if the key fits the storage room. I'll watch the elevator and warn you if the light goes on."

"Got it, Airkool, over and out."
Watson sped out into the hall and darted around the corner.

There was crackling over the speaker.

"I'm at the main target, Airkool. Over and out."

"Just shut up, Watson, and get on with it."

Haydecker hoped her mother didn't come in at just this moment or some confessions would be in order.

To her horror, Haydecker, who had been staring at the elevator light, saw the door to the stairwell open. She had forgotten to pay attention to the stairs.

Through the stairwell door, with a brisk step came Ozzieone, or to be more exact, Mr. Oswald McCaw I. He spotted his son immediately before Haydecker could even get the walkie-talkie to her lips.

Her "Watch out, Oz," was too late.

"What are you doing, son?"

"Oh, hi, Dad." Ozzie left his thumb depressed on the walkie-talkie button so Haydecker would hear the conversation even though the two McCaw's were out of camera range around the corner.

"You know you are not to be messing around these halls. Mr. Bonomolo has been very explicit about children running in the halls. Do you want to get us evicted? Come along home immediately."

Haydecker heard a swat.

"Ow!" It was Oz.

"Talk to you later!" Watson was a little breathless as he signed off, as if he was being rushed down the hall, not quite under his own steam

And speaking of steam, if Mr. McCaw was angry with Ozzie, Haydecker wondered just what he would say when he saw the 'mac and cheese' for his dinner.

Haydecker vowed she could not send Ozzietwo out alone again. She should have been standing guard and have intercepted Mr. McCaw before he saw what Ozzietwo was doing. She would just have to go too next time. She hoped that in all the excitement, Watson hadn't lost the evidence. Did he still have the key?

The black box crackled again. "It didn't fit, Airkool." Then the walkie-talkie lay on the bed, silent. Haydecker didn't dare pick it up and try to reach Ozzietwo again. She would just have to wait. Would they be able to find the door belonging to the key?

Hercule Poirot was determined. Meanwhile, the famous detective had more immediate problem, language arts homework. She bet Hercule Poirot and Sherlock Holmes never did language homework when there was a 'game afoot.'

Chapter V

"What I want to know, is, what has been happening down there?" Haydecker was on the house phone to Mad Harold down in the lobby of the Towers. "Surely you've picked up some interesting scuttlebutt."

"I've only been here a few minutes, Haydecker, so give me a break. I'll call back in a little while after I make up an excuse and have gone in to see the old man." Harold always referred to Mr. Bonomolo as "the old man" although there wasn't that much difference in their ages.

"Okay, don't forget, though." The transmitter clicked off. Haydecker was disgruntled. No more had been heard from Ozzietwo since Ozzieone had escorted him down the hall. Her mother would not permit a visit this evening from three friends from school, Nan, Diane, and L. C., who wanted her help in planning a class party. She really missed seeing them at school and missed their informative "chats." She was missing lots of the fun stuff of school and none, well not much, of the drudgery. Television programs were all dull and, so far, there had been no action in the foyer. If only something would happen! But mostly, she worried about Ozzietwo and the key. This was a turn-a-around—missing Oz and worrying about him.

Haydecker had worked out a system for keeping track of things. She would watch a TV program for exactly 15 seconds and then flip to the foyer for a five second scan, and then back to her TV program. Of course, during the commercials, she became an expert at timing them and could watch the foyer for more than five seconds. She was pretty sure she wasn't missing much. Frankly, there wasn't much going on, either on the TV or in the foyer.

Her mother had come in twice to complain about the static she created when she pushed the buttons. The radio in the den crackled when Haydecker changed locations.

Oh, mother," it's not hurting anything and besides, if you had let Nan, Linda, and L.C. come over, I wouldn't be so bored."

"Emily Marie," her mother shot back, and Haydecker knew she was getting close to the edge of her mother's patience. Whenever she was called "Emily Marie", it was a sure sign to back off.

"The only reason you're bored is because of the unfortunate occurrence this morning. Now forget it! Put it out of your mind. The detectives will solve the case in due time. You know perfectly well if your friends had come over tonight you would have talked of nothing but murder and not a word about parties. Now quit flipping Wally's buttons all the time or I will shut him down completely." Mrs. Haydecker spun on her heel and left the room. Haydecker make faces at her retreating back, but resisted the urge to punch another button.

The house phone rang and the voice of Mad Harold blared over the line. "You there, Haydecker? Here's all the poop from the lower level. Are you reaaaddddy?" Harold didn't even wait for an answer.

"First, the old man, Bonomolo, is going to have a stroke at any moment. He is sure he will be fired. He's even talking Italian half the time, so, I am not sure what he knows. I have a feeling that he doesn't know much of anything.

"Second, nobody has clue one as to who the girl is. No one answering that description has been reported missing to the police. Of course, she could be from out of town. But then, everyone speculates, 'what was she doing in this building'? Someone in this building must have known her, but no one has come forth. Isn't that suspicious?"

"What about the cause of death; do they know anything yet?"

"Of course, the medical report is not entirely complete, from what I have been able to understand, but it seems that the probable cause is strangulation. But they are having a little trouble settling what time it happened. Usually they can give an approximate time of death. But if they do, it doesn't make any sense."

"How come?"

"Well, if the murder happened last night in the hall, it is certain that someone would have found her. However, the medical evidence of the condition of the body points to it having happened much earlier. So it looks like they are really up in the middle on that one."

"So, how did your test go this morning?" Haydecker and Mad Harold had discussed his exam in his Torts class in a conversation yesterday.

"A piece of cake--I think--I hope--would you believe, a torte!" Mad Harold brayed loudly at his own pun.

"How does it feel to be so smart, Harold?"

"You should talk, Haydecker. I don't see you spending much time with your nose in the books."

"Well, there is quite a bit of difference between law school and the 8th grade--like Tortes and Twinkies!" Haydecker laughed at her own joke.

"Sure, and it depends on whether you are 23 or a lowly, mere 13!"

"Harold Simpson, I am not a 'mere' anything!" Haydecker felt her temper rising and also knew what it was like for Ozzietwo when she baited him. "Keep me posted, won't you?"

"One more thing, Haydecker. There has been this strange man in the building the past few days. Quite a few people remember seeing him. It may be some kind of mass hysteria. Do you remember seeing anyone?"

Haydecker avoided a direct answer to the question. She tried to avoid lying at all times, whenever she could possibly help it. "A man in a black overcoat almost ran down my mom here in the foyer this noon."

"I think he's the one. Be sure to tell the detectives when you see them again. I'll talk to you later, kid." Mad Harold rang off. Haydecker went back to stewing about Ozzietwo and watching the hall. She had had to, as requested, give up her switching back and forth.

The phone buzzer went off at the same time that the elevator light went on. Haydecker moved fast.

"Haydecker here," she answered the phone. Chubb and Sam and Mr. Bonomolo got off of the elevator.

"Hello, Scarecrow, how's the tricks?" Her dad's voice came over the long distance wire.

"Hi, Dad, not too bad." The three men walked across the hall. Chubb and Sam on either side of Mr. Bonomolo, who was talking rapidly and gesturing with both arms.

"Have you solved the murder yet?"

"Not yet, but I've been working on it."

"Scarecrow, I wasn't serious. You keep yours and Wally's noses out of that funny business. Do you hear me? Let me speak to your mother."

"I'll behave, Dad." Haydecker used the intercom, "Dad's on the line, Mom." She switched off.

Mr. Bonomolo and the two detectives were just disappearing down the long hall. Haydecker had missed what they were saying.

She had little time to wonder because, in a few seconds, they reappeared to stand in the center of the hall. Mr. Bonomolo's voice, in its excitement, was three octaves higher than usual. The hall intercom picked up his distinctive voice.

"I don't know! I don't know! I don't know!" Bonomolo's arms raised and lowered to punctuate his sentences. "Why do you think I know anything about this wretched murder. You could see for yourself that the Storage Room hasn't been used for any ulterior purpose or, if the body was left in there, no sign of it is being left. Did you see any marks where it was dragged along?" He headed toward the elevator.

"Relax, Tony, we'll get to the bottom of this," Chubb followed behind him.

"Relax, relax! That's easy for you to say! Just maybe my job depends on this. And now how am I ever going to be able to rent the empty apartment on this floor. And then what? I tell you, you police people don't have the slightest idea. . ." The elevator door closed on his sentence and the shadows of his pumping arms against the stainless steel walls of the elevator were gone.

Chubb and Sam stood for a moment in the center of the hallway looking at one another, neither one saying anything. Then, as if they were one person, they turned and headed toward the Haydecker's door.

Haydecker saw that her mother was off the phone so she let them go ahead and ring the bell so that her mother could answer. Haydecker fervently hoped that Ozzietwo wouldn't pick this time to reappear on the scene.

The two detectives disappeared from the camera's view.

"Emily," Emily's mother appeared at the door with the detectives in tow. "The detectives have a few more questions for us, if you are feeling up to it." The look on her mother's face made Haydecker pretty sure her mother was aware that she wouldn't refuse.

 Mrs. Haydecker drew up chairs for the two men for the second time that day. Woof jumped down from his resting place on the bed and checked the shoes and the pant cuffs of each of the two men. Haydecker was fairly sure that neither of them had a dog. Woof would surely have said something.

The detectives settled into their chairs agreeing to Mrs. Haydecker's invitation to coffee. "Well, Miss Haydecker, just a few more questions before we all turn in for the day." It was Chubb speaking as he tried to casually let his glance drift toward Wally's monitor which showed a picture of an empty foyer.

"We are, at the moment, trying to get more information about a man in a black coat who has been seen around the building today. I understand you saw him in the hall?"

Haydecker explained the encounter when the man had surprised Mrs. Heifitz. Haydecker kept her milk glass in her hand during her description. Deliberately she got a milk moustache, hoping they would be distracted in case she was looking as guilty as she felt.

She knew she should tell about the key in the plant. But she and Ozzietwo were already in too deep to confess without having some evidence so that the detectives wouldn't be too angry. She and Ozzietwo would have to work it out later.

Mrs. Haydecker brought in a coffee tray with more slices of chocolate cake. Haydecker looked at the cake wishfully. She didn't want any, but she wished it were Ozzietwo instead of the detectives who were munching into the double layer loaded with frosting. She was beginning to get a little worried about Ozzietwo. She hoped he hadn't been grounded indefinitely. Sometimes his mother or his father got a little funny and grounded him for months almost for no reason at all. Mostly, however, it would be forgotten in a day or so.

"I don't mind telling you, Lieutenant, that the residents of the building are very nervous over this, especially those of us on the seventh floor. There has certainly been a lot more locking of doors and looking over shoulders today.

"We are making progress, Mrs. Haydecker." Chubb talked with his mouth full. Silent Sam just chewed, with his mouth closed.

"We are still checking on the identity of the dead woman. From appearances, she is not an American. Her clothes look foreign-made, but the labels have all been very clumsily removed so it is difficult to tell for sure until we do some checking. She certainly doesn't fit any of the missing person descriptions we have had in the city in sometime."

"Can either of you give us any information on the man you saw today?"

Mrs. Haydecker could give very few details other than the long black overcoat and the black hat. Haydecker tried to think of some other detail to satisfy their curiosity. She ran back the film of the event in her mind. She saw again the man getting off the elevator.

"He had gloves on," she offered. "And he acted real nervous when he saw Mrs. Heifitz. She nearly lost her buns."

"Buns?" Silent Sam nearly choked.

"Onion rolls. She was bringing me some onion rolls that she had made today. If you get a chance, let her give you one of her onion rolls."

Chubb looked interested.

"Do you remember anything else?" Sam asked the question. Apparently Chubb was still thinking of onion rolls.

"He acted kinda funny." Haydecker volunteered.

"What do you mean, funny?"

"Not funny, ha-ha, but I mean funny, weird. Kind of sneaky like."

Chubb just stared at her and didn't make any marks in his notebook. Haydecker supposed that it would be embarrassing to put acted 'funny, weird' down in the notebook. She would like to have gotten a look at what they were writing. She decided to change the subject.

"Do you know yet how she died?" Haydecker thought that would change the focus of the conversation.

"The medical examiner's report isn't ready yet. But it looks like she was hit on the head with a blunt instrument and then strangled. She didn't die from the blow with the blunt instrument."

Haydecker wondered what a 'blunt' instrument was. That one she would have to look up--people were always being hit with 'blunt' instruments. She had visions of a section of the orchestra filled with strange looking things called 'blunt' instruments. Or saying to her mother, "I am going to play a solo at the school band concert on my 'blunt' instrument."

Haydecker could tell that Sam and Chubb had a few more questions before they could tear themselves out of the apartment. Sam looked at the overflowing bookshelf across the room. Haydecker was a little embarrassed that she hadn't straightened it up like her mother had suggested.

"Wow, you have a lot of books. I suppose you have extra time for reading being in bed so much? What are your favorite books?" That was a lot of questions for Silent Sam.

"Oh," Haydecker, answered thinking she would put a bit of an itch into the detectives, "I kinda like Sherlock Holmes and Agatha Christie and lots of detective stuff. Someday I would like to write a mystery."

Sam and Chubb looked a little uncomfortable and suddenly got up to leave. They still sneaked peeks at the TV monitor as they left the room. The hall had been empty most of the evening. According to Haydecker's calculations everyone but Sherie Gerot was in the for supper hour.

 Chubb and Sam went out the front door and Mrs. Haydecker piled the cups and plates on the tray and returned to the kitchen. Haydecker was alone with Wally once again.

Chapter VI

Haydecker decided to try Ozzietwo on the walkie-talkie once more. Softly she put out the call.

"Watson, Watson, Come in, Watson. This is Hercule calling. Over and out." She thought she would humor him and use CB lingo. She released the button and turned up the volume.

"Hey, Haydecker, Airkool, I mean. Did I ever catch it tonight from my dad. He never comes home at that hour. I have been grounded for the evening which is why I haven't been down. Do you read me, Airkool? Over." Ozzietwo was really warming up to the walkie-talkie stuff.

Haydecker had to admit, it wasn't so bad, and in this case, pretty convenient.

"Hello, Watson, sorry about that! What are you doing now?"

"Sitting in the bottom of my closet to talk to you. I'd really catch it if they knew I wasn't in bed and asleep. It is really good I had that piece of cake at your house. I got no dinner or snack. Of course, I have a few reserve supplies hidden in the back of my closet for just such emergencies." Ozzietwo sounded a little smug and not very hungry. He sounded mostly sorry for himself.

"So what about the key?" Airkool inquired.

"It didn't fit, Haydecker. It must belong to the empty apartment. Shall we try that later tonight? Over."

"Do you think you should risk it? Can you stay awake that long? Over."

"Oh, pooh, Haydecker!" Ozzietwo forgot detecting for the moment. "I've stayed up later than that lots of times. What time can you get out? I'm not gonna go into that apartment alone. We can meet in the hall. Over."

"Mom usually goes to bed a little after Mad Harold comes back from the walk with Woof. We should probably give it about fifteen more minutes. Just to make sure let's say we will meet at midnight. Over."

"Roger, Airkool. Over and out."

"See you later, Watson. Why don't you call me when you are ready to leave the apartment--not on the phone, the walkie-talkie."

For the remainder of the evening the hall was very quiet. The tragedy of the murder seemed to have put a stop to a lot of the coming and going by seventh floor residents. Ozzieone had gone out again. The Browers all came home late. Grace Onken's date brought her home and, to Haydecker's chagrin, they said goodnight out of sight in front of Grace's door. She could have used some romance stuff after all the murder discussion. All in all, it was a quiet evening.

After her last TV program was over, Haydecker pretended to get ready for bed. Woof got restless waiting for Mad Harold and Mrs. Haydecker was thinking of a million reasons to come in and sit and talk. She was restless, too.

"Emily, you'll just have to turn Wally off now." Mrs. Haydecker set a glass of milk down on the bedside table. "You have been glued to that foyer all day. The excitement is over. There is certainly not going to be another murder in the same place tonight. Besides, there is a policeman stationed in the building somewhere. Now, drink your milk."

"You can never tell," Haydecker quipped. "One good turn may deserve another."

"Emily Marie, now!"

Haydecker reached over and snapped the buttons on the console. The screen went dark just as Mad Harold got off of the elevator. Woof lifted his head. Without being told, he rose and silently left the bedroom and went to stand at the front door.

"Good night, now, and sleep well." Mrs. Haydecker kissed her daughter good night, switched off the light and left the bedroom in darkness except for a brief, small glow where the light of Wally's screen had been.

Emily sat back to wait. The red numbers on the clock were her company. She listened to the noises of the apartment building as the residents settled in for the night. One never realized there was so many noises going on around them until you were quiet and stopped to listen, really listen.

A door slammed on the floor below; the dishwashing machine in the Haydecker kitchen ceased whirring; the buzzers of the elevator ended with a clunk; the doors rolled open; Mrs. Haydecker ran water in the bathroom; faintly a TV set could be heard with theme music for the late night talk show.

Woof came back from his walk and pressed his winter-cold muzzle against her arm. Haydecker buried her nose in the fresh air of his coat. She longed to be outside sledding, skating, and sloshing to school with the other kids. Her recovery was slow going. She was the kind of girl who moved a lot faster than this.

Haydecker dozed off for a few minutes and when she awoke the apartment was quiet. She waited until the clock blazed 11:57 and carefully got out of bed and crossed the chilly room to make sure the door was closed tightly. Woof barely stirred. She turned Wally back on and, after checking to see that the hall was empty, dove under the covers with the walkie-talkie.

"Watson, do you read me?" The air crackled with static

There was a long pause. Haydecker tried again.

This time a sleepy voice answered, "Oh, yeah, sure, Haydecker, it's me!"

"Ozzietwo, you were asleep."

"Nope, just resting my eyes a little so I will be fresh."

"Are you still sitting in the closet?"

"Yes, and I don't mind saying that my rear end is getting a little sore from sitting all these shoes and stuff. Can you see? Is the coast clear?"

"All set to go. Be quiet now. I'll meet you in the hall in two minutes. Don't forget the key."

Haydecker pulled on the fuzzy white robe and slippers that had been the only clothes she had gotten for Christmas. The other girls had brought over their great new sweaters and shirts and coats. She ached to be able to put on a new outfit and just go out for a while.

Remembering her flashlight, she left Woof, the wonder watch-dog, snoring, and crept out of the apartment. She carefully fixed the front door from the inside so it wouldn't lock her out. She stood at the door waiting for Ozzietwo; she was ready to dart back inside if need be.

A red-plaid robe streaked around the corner. Ozzietwo was in it and he, thought Haydecker, had been more alert. The black hoods of his eyelids almost completely covered his usually sparkling brown eyes.

"It took you long enough. You're slowing down in your old age, McCaw," she whispered loudly.

"Geez, Haydecker, you haven't been in trouble once already today."

"Well, let's quit standing around the hall jawing."

They scurried to the door of apartment 7A and Ozzietwo, better known on this caper as Watson, produced the key from his red-plaid pocket.

"Don't be all night about it, Oz!" Haydecker felt nervous and exposed standing there in the brightly-lit hall.

"Shut up, Haydecker, you scrunch! If you're so fast, be my guest." He slapped the key into her palm.

Haydecker inserted the key smoothly into the lock. Noiselessly, it turned and the door swung to reveal black rooms beyond. The clunk of the elevator cables sounded as the elevator door prepared to open. Haydecker and Ozzietwo, Hercule and Watson, plunged into the blackness and quickly closed the apartment door behind them as they heard the elevator doors slide open.

"You there, Airkool?" Ozzietwo's voice shook a little; he was out of breath, probably from both excitement and from fear. He would never admit that though.

"Right here, Watson," Haydecker groped around in the dark and finally found the top of Watson's head.

"Geez, it's dark!" Ozzietwo moved closer to Haydecker.

"I have just the thing." Haydecker pulled out the pen flashlight and flipped the switch. The thin pale beam did little more than illuminate the shape of her hand.

"Oh, darn, I forgot to check the batteries."

"See, you aren't always so smart, Haydecker." Ozzietwo was beginning to get his courage back.

"Well, what now?"

"Oh, I never said I was. Well," Haydecker wasn't so sure of 'what' was next either.

"At least we know now that the key fits this apartment. As long as we're here we might as well look around a little. Whoever hid the key must have been doing something in this apartment."

"We're not going to see much with that puny flashlight. Gee whiz, a couple of swell detectives we'd be. Gosh, it's cold in here." Ozzietwo's teeth were beginning to chatter.

"I wonder who left the windows open. Let's look and see if one of them might be broken by vandals." Haydecker shone the faint beam of the light a few paces ahead of them as they shuffled together through the apartment, Ozzie clutching the back of Haydecker's robe.

The apartment consisted of a kitchen, a combination dining and living room, and two bedrooms. The very pale light cast shadows in the kitchen where all the doors to the cupboards and refrigerator were standing open. Windows were standing slightly ajar in the bedrooms and the sliding glass door onto the balcony had been unlocked and pushed open, not far, but enough to significantly affect the temperature in the vacant rooms. That niggled at Haydecker's brain. Why would the door have been opened, especially in the winter.

Ozzietwo and Haydecker stood huddled together, shivering.

"Do you think we ought to close it?" Ozzietwo's whisper seemed loud enough to be heard in the main foyer on first floor.

"Yeah, but be careful of fingerprints. You do it, Oz."

"Sure, you make me do it in case there is any evidence left." Ozzie was more than a little crabby tonight.

Watson carefully took the cloth of his robe and covered his fingers while he shoved the door closed.

"I suppose we are messing around with evidence in a murder case and we will each get twenty years in the pen." Ozzietwo sounded disgusted with their adventure.

"Let's go, Haydecker, and come back when we can see. We should'a thought of it being so dark. We'll be able to sneak in, even during the day, if we are careful."

Haydecker agreed. She was chilled through and felt like she would never get warmed up again.

"OK, Watson, but now we gotta' get out of here without getting ourselves into a jam."

"You're taller. You look through the peep hole and make sure the coast is clear. I'm not tall enough." Ozzie sounded a little more like his old self. "You keep the key until we need it again."

Haydecker looked out the tiny hole in the door. The panorama of the foyer in both directions, to the left, to the right, and she could also see directly down the hall, a view that she missed from her own door. The brief look showed only empty carpet and closed doors.

Haydecker clapped her hand over Ozzietwo's mouth for silence to listen and see if the elevator was in use. There was no tell-tale hum or the clunking of cables. It seemed as if the building was entirely asleep at last.

"OK, go, Oz, and I'll wait here until you are safe inside your door. See you in the morning."

She opened the door just wide enough to let him through and watched through the crack in the door as he sped soundlessly down the hall, his Batman slippers flying at each stride. Just as he was turning the knob on 7F, he gave a wave and a grin of triumph.

Now, she had to get back safely and undetected. She listened again and looked carefully. Nothing, and nobody was in sight. Shivering from the chill in the apartment, she crept into the warm hall, closing the door quietly behind her.

She covered the few steps to her apartment quickly and concentrated on opening the door quietly, having left it unlocked. Just one more step to safety on the other side. But she wasn't quick enough.

Dwight Mohr flung open the door to 7B and was standing there looking at Haydecker with his mouth open in surprise.

A shrill voice came from behind him. "What's more, I don't care whether you ever come back. Maybe I should tell the police that you were out until 4:00 last night."

A hair brush clunked against the sturdy oak of the door frame.

Dwight ducked, still staring at Haydecker.

"What are you just standing there for. . ." Sara Mohr's voice drifted off as she looked around her husband's shoulder.

The three of them, Dwight, Sara, and Haydecker, stood there gaping at one another in the empty foyer. It seemed like no one could think of anything to say.

"Well, goodnight," Haydecker tried as she finally broke the spell. Feeling foolish, but darting into the door as quickly as she could, she stood with her back to the door, breathing heavily, tired, wondering if she could ever get up in the morning. Wondering what in the world was going on with Sara and DD and what they had to do with this case.

"Emily Marie Haydecker!" Her mother sat in the living room, Woof beside her, the living room lights ablaze. "Where have you been at this hour of the night, dressed like that? Not far, I hope."

Haydecker started to mumble something about getting something out of the storage closet.

"No, no don't waste my time in the middle of the night with such feeble excuses. I know that you and Ozzie have been up to something this evening, probably trying to play detective. Now, get to bed immediately and we will discuss this in the morning. No more nocturnal wandering about the building. You're lucky I hadn't called the police yet."

Mrs. Haydecker grasped her firmly by the upper arm and they marched. Haydecker always knew when big trouble was afoot. You marched, even Woof marched, into the bedroom.

Haydecker had intended to stay awake and think things over but she could feel herself rapidly losing her hold on wakefulness. Mrs. Haydecker left the room shaking her head, at the same time, smiling to herself, a smile that she would never have let Haydecker see.

Chapter VII

The next morning the phone woke Haydecker out of a very sound sleep. She heard her mother answer in the kitchen. She wanted to roll over and go back to sleep but she could feel something nagging at the front of her mind. Suddenly, she was wide awake with a start. Last night returned vividly. If only she and Ozzietwo had given the key to the detectives in the first place. She dreaded the confession she was going to have to make to her mother. Then, almost assuredly the detectives would be called in.

But that was not to happen for hours yet.

Haydecker lay in the dark of the early morning, waiting for something to happen. The clock said 6:05. Who would call at that hour in the morning?

Her mother came to the door of the room, a little breathless, buttoning the placket of her nurses uniform. "There is an emergency at the hospital and they are short of nurses to staff the emergency room. It may be a long day. I'll phone when I can. You behave yourself and stay in bed today. Now do you hear, Emily Marie? No more running around the building."

Haydecker nodded. She didn't trust herself not to say something stupid.

"What were you and Ozzie doing out in the hall so late at night?" Mrs. McCaw would have a fit if she knew. "Don't tell me you were solving the murder. I should know better than to ask. Remember when you are pulling those shenanigans that you are sick and Ozzie is just a small boy whose first responsibility is to go to school. He can't stay home in bed this morning."

She leaned over and gave Haydecker a kiss.

"Harold Simpson should be along any minute to walk Woof. Take care." She rushed out of the room and then back in again. "Your lunch is in the oven. Just turn it on for 30 minutes when you are feeling ready"

Haydecker was glad to sink back into quiet and darkness. But she knew it wouldn't last. Woof was getting restless. He knew the walk time was fast approaching. Haydecker had often thought that someone ought to do some research on the internal clocks of dogs.

The door buzzer rang. Haydecker flipped on the hall monitor. It was Mad Harold looking like he had never needed sleep in his life.

She clicked the door open.

"Come, Woof!" The dog was off the bed in mid-snore, covering the distance to the door in one huge leap.

"Haydecker, are you awake? I've got some interesting news when I get back." The door slammed shut behind the man and the dog.

"Simpson, you skunk," Haydecker had quickly turned on the intercom into the foyer. "How can you go off like that and leave me breathless in suspense. How can you do that to a poor, sick girl?"

Mad Harold turned around and faced the camera and made a face, giving a Bronx cheer. He and Woof went to the elevator to wait; one of the two was whistling cheerfully.

Harold's announcement had suddenly made Haydecker more wide awake. She went into the bathroom to wash her face and brush her teeth. She wondered how Ozzietwo was doing this morning. Or, she wondered, who was feeling worse, he or Watson.

Harold and Woof buzzed to reenter the apartment after what seemed like hours had elapsed. The clock said twenty minutes.

Haydecker supposed it was cold out this morning. Since she had been sick, she almost never thought about the weather. She didn't even have a winter coat this year. She missed throwing snowballs and splashing in puddles and tobogganing on Morton's Hill.

"OK, Harold Simpson, get in here and give me the whole scoop on everything you know."

Woof took off for the kitchen and a drink of water and his breakfast which Mrs. Haydecker would have put out before she left.

Harold stood in the doorway, "Everything, Haydecker, even 'Torts'? I'll have to be quick, as I am past time to go on duty and everyone is really touchy about stuff these days.

"Tony came in late last night and said that the police are really puzzled about exactly when the murder was committed. Usually they can tell from the autopsy but this one really has them stumped. It seems as though the girl had been dead for some time but there isn't much sign that the body had started to deteriorate. It is almost as if the lady was frozen and then thawed out. The question is, who would have a freezer big enough to store a frozen body? Or who would want to and why?" Harold sniffed and shook his head.

Harold turned to go. "You OK, Haydecker? I suppose all this talk about dead bodies before breakfast makes you a little squeamish. Like a girl. Come to think of it, I'm feeling a little yucky. I'll talk to you later and keep you posted. Be sure to lock behind me. I won't be going to class this morning so I will be around." His voice drifted off into the living room and out the door.

Haydecker grabbed the walkie-talkie, "Can you hear me, Watson, wake up!" Only static came over the line.

"Ozzietwo, come to, now!"

There was a click and the static disappeared.

"Darn it, Haydecker, lay off will you and let a fellow get some sleep. I don't want to be a detective this early in the morning."

Ozzietwo clicked out.

"I mean it, wake up, Oz. I have some important news."

"What is so important this early in the morning."

"I can't tell you over this thing. Get your rear down here soon. That's an order, Watson."

"Blow it out your ear, Haydecker."

 Haydecker smiled. It seemed clear that Ozzietwo got a little crabby when he missed his sleep. She was glad she didn't teach fifth grade at school. Maybe he could convince Mrs. McCaw that he was sick, although she wasn't too amused by Ozzietwo staying at home. Haydecker often thought it was because she didn't want him under foot.

Haydecker looked up at the television monitor. She had heard a click over the sound system. This time of the morning was ordinarily the time for a lot of going but not much coming. Not too often did someone get off of the elevator. The click had signaled, not the elevator, but the opening of the door at the end of the foyer.

The door next to the elevator, the door to the stairwell, opened slowly. Haydecker waited. The door remained open. Haydecker waited. She could see some slight movement in the dark shadows of the stairwell, but she could not see who was doing the moving. The door still remained open.

Then, Haydecker could hear a door open down the long arm of the hall which she could not see with her camera. Someone had come out of one of the apartment, either the Browers, the McCaws, the single ladies: Golda, Grace, or Sherrie, or it might be the General.

Haydecker strained looking for someone to appear. The door to the stairwell had closed to a small slit, just big enough for an eye to keep a lookout in the foyer and hall. Someone was standing down the hall signaling to the person in the stairwell.

Haydecker waited, straining her eyes at the grainy, black and white picture on the TV monitor. Finally she could stand it no longer. She turned up the amplifier as far as I would go on the sound system to the hall. She shouted into the microphone.

"You are being watched. I know everything."

The stairwell door slammed immediately. There was a slight shadow of a movement from down the long hall. A door clicked open and then closed.

Haydecker's heart was pounding. Why had she done that? Now, someone, probably someone who had committed murder knew that she could see what was happening in the hall. Worse, they now thought she knew something she didn't know. Would they try to keep her from telling; wouldn't they get rid of a witness if they could? She lay back on her pillows looking at Woof. In a pinch, she wondered, would he be any help against a determined murderer?

Impossible as is sounded, she must have dozed off. "Haydecker, let me in!" It was Ozzietwo at the door, dressed in his school clothes, but looking only about half awake.

"Are you alone, Oz?"

"Of course, I'm alone. Who would I be with?

"Look around carefully, will you."

"Geez, Haydecker, what's the matter with you. How come you are so touchy all of a sudden? Is there something out here?"

Suddenly, Ozzietwo got the message. He looked around him and huddled nearer the door. "Lemme in, Haydecker, come on, quick!"

"OK, it's open." She flipped the lock button and Ozzietwo darted into the living room. She resecured the lock.

Ozzietwo raced into the bedroom and threw himself onto the bed. "What's happened, Haydecker?"

"Oz, I just did something dumb!"

"Oh, no, not you, Haydecker, you never do anything dumb," he shot back at her sarcastically.

Haydecker filled him in on the past few minutes.

Ozzietwo listened, wide-eyed.

"Well," said Watson, with a half a grin, "I gotta admit. That is dumb. Airkool, it ain't elementary this time."

Ozzietwo giggled nervously.

Haydecker stared at him. Ozzietwo stared right back. They could hardly wait for what they would discover next. Not only was the mystery thickening but they were snap-dab in the middle of the stew.

Chapter VIII

The apartment was quiet that morning. Even Woof did not seem to be much company. Haydecker tried to concentrate on school but found herself wishing that Ozzietwo had skipped and stayed home. She switched Wally frequently to glare at the silent elevator and the closed door beside it. Now, someone out there thought she knew who had done the murder. She knew that sooner or later her big mouth would get her into trouble. The time had come.

Haydecker dozed off. It had been a short night. But if Emily Marie Haydecker or Hercule Poirot, had been awake, she would have seen a man come into the foyer, a man wearing a long, black coat. She would have seen him disappear from her view into apartment 7A.

The doorbell shattered both Haydecker's and Woof's sound sleep. Woof sat very alertly while Haydecker rolled over and punched the monitor to the on position. It was Joseph Plimpton, Haydecker's "itinerant" teacher, hired by the school to visit several times a week to assist her with her school work.

Since she was hooked into the school by TV, she usually asked all of her questions over the air. But, as Mr. Plimpton was fond of saying, "The law is the law." So he continued to visit her and they talked of other things besides math and social studies and language arts.

Mr. Plimpton stood there at the door, smiling expectantly, an extra chin escaping from over the collar of his coat. Mr. Plimpton made up in chins what he lacked in height.

Haydecker punched the button, "Come on in, Mr. Plimpton. Are you sure you are alone?" Haydecker was ashamed at herself trying to make him uncomfortable.

Joseph Plimpton glanced around the foyer nervously. There were several things Mr. Plimpton was not long on, and one of them was courage, another two were height and sobriety. But Haydecker had to admit that of all the people she knew, Mr. Plimpton was one of the smartest and knew a lot of things about a lot of things. She could look forward to interesting conversations whenever he was around.

Wiskr entered the room. Haydecker had long ago named him "Wiskr" for the intelligence test he had once given her (WISC-R which stood for the Wechsler Intelligence Scale for Children-Revised). The name "WISKR" had stuck.

When "Wiskr" entered the room Haydecker got a strong odor of BRUT (Mr. Plimpton was hardly the BRUT type), and LAVORIS, and cigarettes, and somewhere under it all she caught a slight whiff of some unknown substance. Mr. Plimpton took off his warm trench coat and plumped down in the wingback chair. With his trench coat off he didn't look quite so much like a tan, over-stuffed sausage.

"Well, now, before you tell me all about this murder business, are you having any difficulties with your homework? First things first, Emily." Mr. Plimpton always said "first things, first," too.

Haydecker, alias Emily, did admire "Wiskr" for sticking to business. It was always studies before any other conversation. She was usually thankful that she didn't need much help with the lessons.

She dragged her school books off the shelf on the bedside table and showed him the partially done homework.

"Your teacher is not displeased with the quality of your work but she thinks you don't always pay attention in class. Could such a thing be possible?" Wiskr was only acting serious and stern. They had often talked about how difficult it was going to be for her to go back to school where she had to pay full-time attention again.

"Now we have dispensed that that business portion of our visit. Do you feel that you have been duly chastised for not paying attention in class?" He was only doing his duty sounding teacherly.

Haydecker nodded. They always had that conversation just in case anyone asked.

"Tell me what you know about this murder which allegedly occurred on this floor of your building?"

Haydecker proceeded through a recitation of all the details beginning with the first morning and the crowd assembled around the body under the plaid blanket. She would confess later to Ozzietwo that there were a few details which she left out--like finding the key and the trip last night to the empty apartment. Mr. Plimpton was a stickler for law and order. Had he heard that, a report would have had to have been made.

Mr. Plimpton was also very inquisitive and had a tendency to ask interesting questions. He observed many things that other people didn't notice. Haydecker thought that in that regard he was a good role model.

"So how was she killed?"

"Strangled, I think. But Mad Harold says there is some problem deciding when she died. I wonder why? What do you know about dead bodies and autopsies, Mr. Plimpton?"

Mr. Plimpton cleared his throat. As it turned out Mr. Plimpton knew something about dead bodies. Haydecker knew she was going to get the whole encyclopedia. This was one of those times she didn't mind. Haydecker often thought it was too bad he wasn't still a regular school teacher rather than this itinerant teacher (or what Ozzietwo called the "ignorant" teacher).

"Well, a lot of factors can influence the condition of a corpse and how long it takes rigor mortis to set in."

Haydecker shivered slightly. The sight of the woman's body lying on the hall carpet still kept nipping at the corners of her mind, even when she worked hard to ignore those mental pictures.

"The condition of the victim prior to death can be very important as well as the environment at the time of death. For example, did the murder occur in a very warm climate and did the body remain there? It is also true that. . . " Mr. Plimpton's voice droned on but Haydecker's mind had snagged on the idea of a warm room. She interrupted, "What about a cold room? What would be the result in that case?" She was still shivering from Ozzietwo's and her late night foray into 7A. It had been cold. Suppose that the murder had occurred in 7A.

Wiskr was glad to oblige. "It would, of course, slow down the deterioration of the body. It is the same principle as cooling or freezing food. I'm sure you have heard of recent attempt to freeze people before they die. The intent is to thaw them out later on. There is a name for it which escapes me at the moment. Cryogenics or something."

"Why would anyone want to?" All this was giving Haydecker the "willies." She couldn't see much future in it.

"Oh, it could be that someone is sick and they are frozen with the idea that someone will thaw them out when a cure for their disease is discovered. Or, maybe in the 21st Century, the secret of eternal life will be discovered. Then, they could be defrosted and live forever." Plimpton made a face.

Haydecker wondered if he was interested in being frozen. She wondered if old Wiskr was enjoying life--or maybe he would be frozen and come back later when there was a short cut around his problems.

Wiskr's voice droned on about the advantages and disadvantages of being frozen. Haydecker was itching to get back into 7A and look around for possible clues. Suppose, just suppose, that the woman had been murdered in 7A and stored there. Suppose the murderer, caught in the act of trying to get the body into the elevator, had dropped it in the middle of the hall when he had heard someone coming.

Haydecker's mind wandered further. Just suppose that there was other evidence in the empty apartment, a clue to the motive of the crime or to why all this had taken place here in this building on this floor and was the basis of operations.

Mr. Plimpton was in the middle of his parting speech when Haydecker came back to reality. "And so, Emily Marie, if you have no further need of my expertise," the parting speech was the same every time, "or my services, I shall make my departure. I trust that you will remember me to your gracious parents."

Sometimes, Haydecker thought, Mr. Plimpton sounded like a gentleman who had stepped out of a story from the last century. One of those stories by Charles Dickens or somebody like that. Haydecker always thought he was just a little too educated to be an outbound teacher. Maybe that's why you drank, because you knew too much.

Haydecker watched the clock. The morning was just creeping by. There were five hours left until it was time for Ozzietwo to come home from school. She had never thought she would look forward to seeing Ozzietwo come home. Woof snored in his sleep and

Haydecker snuggled down into her pillows and stared at the empty hall on Wally's monitor. Everything was boring.

Haydecker, jumped, startled. She had fallen asleep. Without her seeing anything at all, there was a lot of activity in the hall. Grace Onken was at the door pushing the buzzer to the Haydecker's apartment. The elevator light was blinking. The General has just rounded the corner and was marching stiffly across the lobby with his heavy silver-headed cane crooked over his arm.

"Come in, Miss Onken, the door is open." Haydecker felt a little uncomfortable. She had never before exchanged more than a brief 'hello' with this school teacher who shared an apartment with Sherrie Gerot. Haydecker had heard her parents speculating about how Grace Onken could afford to live in the Towers on her fifth grade teacher's salary since she hadn't been teaching very long.

"Just follow my voice back to the bedroom." Haydecker shouted. Woof's head was up and his coat was all abristle at the back of his neck.

It was several seconds before Grace Onken appeared in the doorway. Haydecker tried to straighten up the corners of the covers before the guest entered her room.

Grace Onken paused in the doorway. She was dressed in a faded blue sweat suit. Little tendrils of wet hair clung to her hairline. She looked nervous and scared and Haydecker wondered what she was doing home from school today. She really didn't look sick.

"Hello, Emily Marie," her voice was low.

"Hello, Miss Onken." Then Haydecker didn't say anything more, mostly because she didn't know what to say. She began to wiggle inside wondering what had brought on this visit. She had the chilling thought that it might have something to do with what she had said this morning. What if Miss Onken was the villain?

"I hope you don't mind my dropping in like this, but I had a couple of questions that I wanted to ask you." Miss Onken couldn't seem to take her eyes off of Wally.

"If you don't mind my asking, what in the world is that thing?"

"Wally is kind of like a baby sitter and a watch dog when I am here alone in the daytime. I'm not supposed to get up to answer the door or anything." Sure, Haydecker, announce to her that you are here alone. Haydecker launched into her explanation of Wally while together they watched Chubb and Sam as the two detectives examined the carpet in the foyer once more.

"Please won't you sit down, Miss Onken?" Haydecker remembered her manners. She could just hear her mother nudging her along.

Miss Onken sat on the very edge of the wingback chair, looking as if she might, at any moment, fly across the room and perch on the bureau.

"Please call me Grace." Miss Onken smiled nervously, "I guess we don't really know each other very well even though we have lived here on the same floor for quite a while." Somehow Haydecker was having an awful time imagining a school teacher being nervous. She thought that they were real people too.

Haydecker supposed that Miss Onken, Grace, was about to see if she couldn't remedy the fact that they weren't acquainted. Haydecker felt like she was being treated the same as the children in Miss Onken's class. She was a first grade teacher. Some primary teachers even talked to adults that way. Elementary teachers and nurses.

Miss Onken, Grace, sat a little farther back on the chair. Haydecker inwardly sighed with relief. At least the school teacher wasn't going to tip over in her chair and fall flat-faced onto the carpet.

Haydecker toyed with the idea of asking Miss Onken, Grace, to call her something other than Emily Marie, or even Emily. But she decided she would wait on that. She would wait to see how much better acquainted Miss Onken, Grace, was interested in getting.

Haydecker watched carefully; Grace Onken's small hands fiddled with the zipper on the jacket of her red and white and blue sweat suit.

Miss Onken, Grace, leaned forward and started to speak. Wally's buzzer was so loud that both of them jumped, even Haydecker who was used to hearing it. Woof cried out low in his throat, again awakened from his nap. A glance at the screen showed Haydecker that Chubb and Silent Sam were at the door again.

Miss Onken, Grace, jumped to her feet. "Oh, my, I wonder what they want. Who do you suppose they suspect?"

Haydecker spoke into the transmitter. "Come in." She activated the door lock.

"Well, I must be going." Miss Onken, Grace made a swift path to the door. "I'll drop by and see you another time when the police aren't pestering you. Nice talking to you, Emily Marie." She was gone before Haydecker could reply.

Haydecker could hear mumbling in the living room as Miss Onken, Grace, passed Chubb and Sam in the front of the apartment. Haydecker heard the front door close and watched Miss Onken, Grace, stand for several seconds leaning against the outside of the front door. She had apparently forgotten Wally's all-seeing eye and the fact that Haydecker and then Chubb and Sam were watching her.

Chubb's voice broke the silent vigil, "You and Miss Onken pretty good friends, are you?"

Haydecker knew he was fishing. She stared at him innocently and let him dangle his line in the water. If she didn't know why Miss Onken had come, she sure wasn't about to try and explain it to the two detectives. Let them wonder just like she was going to have to do.

"Oh, not too well. I wonder why she isn't in school today." Haydecker wondered out loud, fishing a little herself.

"Longfellow school, where Miss Onken teaches, is having boiler troubles. All the students and faculty are out for the day. It's too cold even for the faculty to stay in school." Haydecker felt better. At least that mystery was solved.

Chubb looked expectantly at Wally's big eye, "Well, young lady, have you seen anything interesting on that thing since we were here yesterday?"

"No, not much."

"What about the man in the black coat?"

Haydecker felt a lump form in her throat. This was going to be tricky. She didn't usually tell lies. But, some poet said something about telling 'all the truth but telling it slant.' This was going to have to be one of those slant times.

"Yeah, Mad Harold said someone with that description had been around the building and my mother told you she nearly got mowed down by the fellow in the hall down stairs. Do you think he might be the murderer?"

"At this point we just want him for questioning as a person of interest. Now, listen, young lady, if you should see anyone answering this description even if they don't have a black coat and hat on, please let us know immediately. We are looking for a male suspect, about 5' 10" or 11" with dark or sallow complexion. He's not very heavy, maybe 135 pounds, although no one describing him has seen him with the coat off, so we really don't know for sure. He walks with his head partly turned to one side."

"Do you have any idea how old he might be?"

"It is difficult to get any kind of fix on that. We do guess that he is not real old and he is not real young. At any rate, under no circumstances are you to let anyone into the apartment who even remotely answers that description, not even if you are stalling for time to call us. Do you understand?"

Once Chubb had gotten all that said, he relaxed a bit and sat down in the same chair recently occupied by Miss Onken. But instead of perching on its edge as she had done, Chubb slumped back and looked like he was preparing for a long stay. He was probably wishing for some more chocolate cake.

Sam was chewing on a toothpick and staring at Wally, as usual. Haydecker always felt just a little guilty. It was like she had a toy and she wouldn't let the other kid, Sam, play with it. She felt the least she could do would be to offer to let him experiment with the console.

"Would you like me to show you how it works?" Briefly she explained each of Wally's buttons and the capability that went with it. Then she turned him loose.

"Did you say your father built this?"

"Yes, electronics is his business as well as his hobby. He has been threatening to add on to it if I am not better soon."

Chubb entered the conversation, "How soon do you expect that to be?"

"I'm hoping to go back to school after spring break, but my doctor thinks it really won't be until fall--but definitely by fall!" When Haydecker thought about it; fall seemed like forever. And there were any "definites".

"Well, have you made any progress in the murder solution?" Haydecker needed to change the subject. She thought she might as well find out as much as she could so she could report to Mad Harold and Ozzietwo. She needed to make staying home count for something.

"We only know that the victim was not an American and there is a great possibility that she may be from Amsterdam in the Netherlands. You wouldn't happen to know if anyone here on this floor is Dutch in background or has friends or relatives living there. Or maybe, someone on this floor has recently visited in the Low Countries?"

"Not anyone I can think of. How could you know that she was from Amsterdam?"

"Whoever had taken her handbag and taken the labels from her clothing, had forgotten to check inside her shoes or that she was wearing a money pouch which contained both Dutch and American currency."

"What was in her shoes? Usually people don't carry any type of identification in their shoes. At least, normal people don't."

Haydecker was really getting interested. "Not a normal situation, huh?"

Chubb responded secretively, "I'm not at liberty to say precisely what it was. Just keep your ears and eyes open for a Dutch connection.

Wally screeched and squawked. Woof lifted his head and gave Silent Sam a disgusted look. Sam stepped back from the console a little embarrassed.

"Come on, partner, quit fooling around with that thing and let's get some lunch. Goodbye, Miss Haydecker, keep alert and be careful."

Finally it was lunch time.

Haydecker wondered briefly, over her lunch-time noodle soup, as she watched the noon news, whether she ought to call Miss Onken, Grace, and see if she could get to the bottom of whatever brought her to the apartment for a visit. It was a certain thing that she had thought better of it when the two detectives had shown up at the door. Haydecker decided on the path of discretion. Better not get too nosey. It could get awfully unhealthy. And frankly, for her part, she had had enough of this being sick. She would just wait Miss Onken, Grace, out. The noon news was uninformative, only reporting things Haydecker already knew; that the murder investigation was on-going but that they were making progress and blah, blah, blah.

Haydecker reflected that she also knew several things that Marcia Fridley from the WBBM noon news did not know: the young woman who had been found dead, was from Amsterdam and the murder had not been committed in the foyer of the seventh floor of the Towers. But, Haydecker's list of questions was getting longer and longer.

She ripped a page from the spiral bound note book that contained her math work for tomorrow. She felt a little twinge of guilt that she had not paid enough attention to her studies. But then, wasn't she pretty well finished with her homework? And if she did too much more now, she would be bored stiff this evening.

She listed:
1. Where had the murder been committed?

2. Why was the body left in the middle of the hall at that early hour of the morning?

3. What connection with Amsterdam did this dead woman have with someone on this floor?

4. Why was it so important to the murderer to remove all traces of the identity of the woman?

5. Why had she been murdered?

6. Who on the seventh floor was involved?

Chapter IX

Haydecker knew that if she could just figure out the motive for the murder, all of the other answers would fall into place. She pondered and thought and thought and pondered and decided that what she needed to do was to check out the empty apartment again. It was a quiet time of day in the hall. After lunch, both Golda Heifitz and Mrs. Brower had gone out dressed as though they were gone for an afternoon of shopping or visiting. With the exception of Grace Onken, almost everyone else was at work. She had, however, forgotten the General. He had gone out earlier in the day. Usually he took several constitutional walks on days when it was fit to be out and about.

Haydecker found the key to 7A in her bed stand. She had stuffed it in the back of the drawer so it would not be noticed in case her mother had an occasion to open that drawer. It looked harmless enough--like just another lost key.

"You stay here for a while, Woof! I'll be back in a few minutes. More importantly, don't talk to anyone or let anyone in while I am gone." She ruffled his fur. She pulled on the long, warm outdoor socks over her bed socks and slipped into jeans and a sweatshirt on top of her pajamas. She still remembered very clearly the cold blast of air that swirled around them as she and Ozzietwo huddled in the empty apartment. At least it wouldn't be dark.

The hall was empty as she pocketed the key to her own door. She listened, standing motionless as she could. Her own breathing seemed to roar. She could hear no sounds from any of the apartment or from the elevator shaft or the stairwell. All the doors remained tightly closed.

Grasping the key with more courage than she felt, Haydecker marched over to 7A. The key again fit smoothly in the lock and the door sprung open at a touch of the knob. She was inside rapidly. She stood inside the door gasping for breath. Her heart wouldn't quite thumping.

The apartment certainly looked different than it had last night by the light of a flashlight, a very dim flashlight. It didn't take nearly so much courage to come in the daylight, even if she had had Ozzietwo for company last night. He would be furious with her for coming without him this afternoon. She just felt that she couldn't wait. There was too much traffic in the foyer in the evening. She knew for certain that neither one of them could stay awake for a second late night visit.

"Okay, Haydecker," sometimes it didn't seem so lonely if she occasionally talked to herself. "Let's go after this systematically. Start in the bedroom and work out toward the kitchen."

The smaller of the two bedrooms had no drapes, no furniture, no carpet and was only distinguished by a correspondingly empty closet. The whole room was more empty than any room Haydecker could ever remember having been in. She wondered if anyone had ever inhabited the room since the Towers was built two years ago.

Across the hall from the small bedroom was the larger of the two. It, too, yawned emptily. However, here were evidences of inhabitation at one time or another. Litter lay in the corner; there were scuff marks on the walls, a closet door stood partly ajar, a few hangers hung crookedly over the bar. Haydecker pulled the closet door all the way open to let the daylight in.

A black object lay toward the back of the closet.

The sight was so unexpected that Haydecker had to stifle the impulse to run. She imagined for a moment that it was furry and moving. What's more, it had a long tail. She held herself rigid and stared closely. It wasn't moving.

She stepped back to side of the doorway to let more light into the recess of the closet. Then she moved closer. It definitely wasn't moving.

Haydecker inched closer. The object, seen in the best of the light, was a lady's handbag, black with a long black strap. She pulled it out and took the handbag to the window to examine it.

As nearly as she could tell, the handbag was made of plastic. The outside was cracked where the handle was sewn into the material. It was badly scuffed with long, grey streaks running along its sides.

Haydecker hefted it. It certainly felt like it had something in it. The sides bulged, particularly on one side.

She clicked the clasp and peered inside. It was stuffed with bits of material, a handkerchief, some make-up and what looked like a wallet.

Haydecker stood absolutely still, but her hands were shaking. It suddenly occurred to her that the handbag certainly must belong to the dead woman.

She wanted to throw down the handbag and flee from the apartment as fast as she could. . .but curiosity got the better of her. Besides, she would never be able to face Ozzietwo with all her talk of detection, and tell him that she hadn't looked inside.

She dumped the contents of the handbag out on the windowsill in order to take inventory. The little scraps of material were labels but not from any stores or companies that Haydecker knew about. The handkerchief was monogrammed with a simple ES in the corner. A folder with UNITED Airlines in bold red, white and blue on its cover came out next. There was a passport and finally the wallet.

Haydecker was about to open the passport. Her hands trembled. She was concentrating so hard on her discoveries that she almost missed the mumble of voices and the click of a key in the door.

Suddenly she felt her stomach tighten. She felt herself get hot all over. She hardly took time to think. And then her only thought was to run. Had these people already killed someone?

She swept the contents into the open mouth of the bag and in almost the same motion flung it back into the closet.

On the verge of going into the closet herself, she thought of the wonderful emptiness of the closet in the smaller room next door. She could see in her mind, the unlived, unoccupied look it presented. It seemed safer because no one had thrown a handbag into it.

She was glad for her stocking feet on the hard wood floor of the small bedroom. She dashed into the closet and closed the door but not quite all the way. She had to be able to hear if they were coming in here.

The voices got louder. Haydecker strained to hear what was being said. She could only hear snatches of what sounded like two male voices. They grew louder as they neared the bedroom door.

Haydecker held her breath.

The moment passed. The voices receded into the other bedroom. Haydecker widened the crack in her closet door and pressed her ear as closely to it as possible.

"Well, if you hadn't been so blasted slow, we could have avoided all this trouble. Don't you. . ." The voice faded away as if it had turned from the door.

"It ez one of zose unfortunate. . ." this voice also rumbled away into a murmur. That voice's owner, as nearly as Haydecker could tell, was not an American. He sounded like some of those Ambassadors or Diplomats that sometimes were on the TV. She wasn't ever sure which country was which.

There was something about the other voice that rang a bell in her memory. It was a voice she had heard before, but not often enough for her to recognize it like this.

The voices came closer again. Haydecker stood as still as she could. She itched everywhere.

"You take this handbag and get rid of it!"

"Non, non, nevair me! Not in broad daylight, I carry a handbag. What you think of? You are, perhaps, crazy!"

"It should never have been left here in the first place. Nor should we be here together at this time of day. Put the handbag where we put the other stuff and we will return for it sometime when one or the other of us won't be seen. Take some of the items, the most damaging ones and destroy them. I am certainly not going to have them found in my apartment. It is not incriminating evidence here."

"We will meet back here when I have the goods. I will leave a note in the usual place. We must, we must, I repeat, be ever vigilant. You can't tell who may be watching or where. There is a possibility that we may already have been discovered by the wretched girl who stays home from school all day. This building should never. . ." the voice faded again.

Haydecker had no doubt about who was being spoken about when one of the men had made mention of "wretched girl" and she felt herself go all hot and then all cold. It seemed as if she had been imprisoned in this closet for three days; her legs, her arms, everything seemed to ache. She wondered why it had seemed such a good idea to come over here. At once she wished that Ozzietwo was with her and at the same time she was glad he wasn't in this pickle with her. If only someone knew she was here.

Haydecker listened carefully to the sounds from the outer rooms of the apartment. It sounded like they were banging something in the kitchen. Was it the refrigerator? She must have been mistaken. Then, there were no more noises except for a click that well could have been the front door.

Haydecker stood silently in the closet. It seemed as though her ears would fall off; she was trying to tune in to the whole apartment building. She could hear the water in the pipes, the frequent whoosh of the furnace blowers; the far-away clanking of the elevator. But no voices. And certainly no noises from the apartment.

Haydecker took a deep breath and stepped out of the closet. She stopped again.

Again, no noises, no sounds of human presence.

She stifled the urge to race out of the apartment. The front door looked at her invitingly. But, she reasoned, at this point, there was no hurry. She was probably safe for the rest of the day. Probably.

She glanced into the kitchen. It was a small cubicle equipped with a refrigerator, stove, and a few small cupboards. All the doors stood gaping open. Haydecker peered into each of the cupboards and the stove. Crumbs, bits of paper lay gracelessly inside the cupboards. Spots of charred food were crumbled on the oven floor. The refrigerator door, unlike the other doors in the kitchen, was closed. She tried to remember if it had been open before. She opened it and took a quick look. It was empty too.

Carelessly, Haydecker pulled open the very bottom drawer marked MEAT. There, like a piece of blackened beef, lay the handbag she had found in the closet. It didn't move this time either. She was going to get a second chance to look at the contents.

Like moving in a dream, Haydecker opened the handbag once again. Again it clicked promisingly. The contents were seriously reduced. The passport was gone, as was the airline ticket. The wallet remained but contained only a few foreign looking bills. As far as Haydecker knew, at this time, the girl was still only ES, but here was, if not proof, at least a strong suggestion that the unfortunate young woman was ES from the Netherlands.

If only she had had another minute or two when she had first discovered the handbag. She had been only seconds from discovering the identity of its owner and perhaps the girl.

Haydecker put the handbag back in the drawer and went to the door. She listened into the foyer again. She closed her eyes, wondering why you could hear so much better when you couldn't see. Then she wondered if the opposite was true and you could see better when you couldn't hear. Why, she wondered, didn't the senses complement each other? Why wouldn't it be a double whammy? She tried to think of an experiment to test the whole idea.

She heard nothing at the door so she peeked out through a crack. There was no activity. She put her head out to check the elevator light. It was dark.

Quickly Haydecker was at her own door, breathing hard, and thinking she had never moved so fast in her life, except maybe last night with Ozzietwo. Shaking, she tried to put her keys in the lock. It wouldn't fit and wouldn't fit and wouldn't fit. She leaned her head against the door. What was the matter with it?

She closed her eyes and took a deep breath. Then she opened her eyes again to look down in frustration at the key in her hand. It said 7A.

No wonder!

She dug in her pocket and pulled out the other key, the once marked 7C. It moved in the lock and she was safe at home.

Woof was waiting by the door. He sat alertly looking at her accusingly. She could almost hear him scolding!

"Oh, come on, Woof! I wasn't gone that long. Let's crawl back into bed. That is enough of that!"

They headed into the bedroom. Haydecker stopped beside her closet and carefully threw her jeans, sweatshirt and socks way back in the corner of the closet. Her mother would wonder if they were put away.

Haydecker slipped into bed under the warm covers. She was tired. Woof leapt up beside her and settled into his usual place, leaning against her feet. His breathing became even and regular as he nestled his chin into his outstretched paws. The afternoon sun shone only dimly through the drawn blinds.

Only moments later, Sylvia Haydecker returned from the hospital, let herself into the apartment with her key. She paused and listened to the stillness. Moving down the hall to her bedroom, she glanced into Haydecker's room. All the occupants were fast asleep. She smiled and continued down the hall.

Haydecker slept through the remainder of the afternoon, through her father's telephone call from the airport, through Ozzietwo's breathless visit at the front door. His face fell when he was told to come back later.

Haydecker awoke feeling as tired as if she hadn't slept at all. The hall door was banging and a loud voice caused Woof to rouse, too. He went out into the living room to see what was happening.
"Scarecrow, are you home?"

"What do you mean, am I home?" Haydecker shouted back. "Nobody is more at home than I am." She breathed a sigh of relief that he couldn't read her mind about the little "not-at-home" adventure of the afternoon. Her mother hadn't even given her a talking to about last night. Maybe she would have forgotten it. Haydecker doubted it. Her mother had a long and healthy memory.

"Well, Scarecrow, what's new in your life? Did you miss your old man?" George Haydecker threw his canvas travel bag into the corner and sat down on the edge of the bed. He looked tired and smelt of cigar smoke and diesel fuel and winter. Haydecker was glad to see him. She returned his hug. He seemed solid and ordinary and usual. She hoped she had dreamed a nearly empty purse in a refrigerator drawer and a man in a black coat and a woman with blond hair on the foyer floor.

"Things are about as usual. How was your trip?"

Her father usually had some interesting story to tell about his business trips. Haydecker sometimes wondered if he didn't make up some of the tales he told or, at least, "fancy" them up a little bit to entertain her because she wasn't able to go anywhere. Usually his most outrageous stories would begin with, "Wait'll you hear what happened. . ." but Haydecker was destined to wait for his rendition of his latest story because just as he got to "happened" who should happen into the bedroom but Ozzietwo. He burst in.

"Oh, boy, Haydecker! Hi, Mr. Haydecker! How'ya doing?" He bounced up on the bed beside Haydecker and her father.

"Hi, yourself, Oz. How's it going with you? Have you been keeping your nose clean while I've been gone?"

Haydecker looked quickly at Ozzietwo. While he was usually pretty swift, he couldn't keep the pained look from his face. He started to speak and then a frog got caught in his throat. He started coughing. Ozzietwo fell off the bed.

Haydecker smiled to herself. She should have known she could trust Ozzietwo to create a diversion. Maybe he would be a great sprinter and then, again, maybe he would be another Sidney Poiter or James Earl Jones.

Mr. Haydecker picked Ozzietwo up by the back of his belt and pounded him on the back of his red polo shirt. Strangle-faced and gurgling, Ozzietwo began to recover, slowly very slowly, but he began to recover.

"Think you'll make it, Oz?" Mr. Haydecker was trying hard not to smile, but he wasn't succeeding very well. He apparently decided a swift exit was the best thing. "Well, I'll leave you two to your business and go talk to your mother. Emily, is it OK if I leave my suitcase here for a minute?"

"Sure, unless stuff crawls out of it." Haydecker glanced at the bag in the corner. It was covered with tags from the airport and stickers from cities her father had visited. A thought struck her. What if someone had traveled to Amsterdam. Might not they still have some tags on their luggage?

"Hey, Oz, wait 'til you hear what I have been up to today. You won't believe this!"

Haydecker proceeded to tell Ozzietwo, describing, in detail, moment by moment, her whole afternoon adventure. Ozzietwo's eyes kept getting wider and wider.

"Geez, Haydecker," he exclaimed, punctuating the end of each of her sentences with his "Geezs."

For a few moments or three, Ozwald P. McCaw II didn't have very much to say, which was certainly an unusual occurrence for him.

But it wasn't long before he recovered his courage and his voice. "Boy, Haydecker, I shoulda been with you. I woulda tackled 'em both. We coulda captured them and then we'd a both been heroes." Visions of great deeds danced in Ozzietwo's head.

Haydecker didn't dare suggest that he probably would have been as scared as she had been. She and Ozzietwo would have plenty of scary times in the future as they grew up. And probably none of them from here on out would have to do with murderers.

"Well, whadda we do now, Haydecker? Shall we go back there tonight?" Ozzietwo was sounding pretty brave, knowing that he probably wouldn't have to follow through on that suggestion. At the same time, he was a little hurt at having missed the great adventure of the day.

"We have to keep an eye on the plant for a new note which we can intercept. Maybe we can throw their plans off if we take the note. Meanwhile, we have got to get into the luggage room. Who's got a key?"

"I don't know." Ozzietwo had recovered full voice and his composure. "I think my parents have one. Do you want me to go see?"

"Yes, we have to get into the luggage room. But can you get a key without arousing suspicion?"

"Nah, they will think I am going in there just to mess around. I have done that a couple of times in the past. I have to have a good excuse to be in there."

"Tell them you want to help my dad put his luggage away and we can't find our key. When you get in there, look for a suitcase with a tag on it that says 'Amsterdam' or the initials ALM."

"Haydecker, I can't even spell Amsterdam. You had better come along."

"It is high time you learned to pronounce Amsterdam and spell it too. Here, I'll write it on a piece of paper for you." She took out a small slip of paper from the night stand and wrote the letter for him. He was out the door like a flash. Ozzietwo was no scholar but he certainly was a man of action.

Would Ozzietwo find a clue in the Storage Room?

Chapter X

Haydecker was allowed to come to dinner in the dining room in honor of her father's return from his trip. He did regale the family with descriptions of persons he had met or jokes from the speakers at his conference. Haydecker was having a grand time in spite of the fact that she was still tired around the edges. This detection was very exhausting.

Her father concluded the account of his trip, "I shared a cab with Oliver Brower coming in from the airport. What a coincidence. He really seemed agitated by this murder on the floor."

"Oh, where had Mr. Brower been?" Mrs. Haydecker questioned.

Haydecker sat up, listening.

"He didn't say. He had, however, been through customs because he was complaining about the time it took."

"Hah!" Haydecker thought. "At last! A suspect!" She finished her milk, wondered how to find out where Mr. Brower had been.

The doorbell buzzed and before either of the elder Haydeckers could put down their napkins, a voice bellowed, "Airkool, are you here?" The elder Haydeckers exchanged a puzzled look. The door slammed and the muffled thud of feet could be heard pounding into Haydecker's room.

Louder this time, the voice roared, "Hey, Haydecker!"

"Here, Oz, in the dining room."

Haydecker no sooner got the words out of her mouth than Ozzietwo burst into the room and screeched to a halt at

Haydecker's corner of the table. A faint sprinkle of perspiration dotted his forehead and his upper lip. Oswald P. McCaw II's eyes sparkled and a brief smile played around his lips.

It was clear to Haydecker that Ozzietwo was up to something--or on to something--or into something. She hoped that wasn't equally clear to her parents.

"Hello, again, Ozzie, it is really good to be seeing so much of you for a change. How about some dessert? Mrs. Haydecker has a wonderful apple crisp dessert here, just warm from the oven. I hope you'll join us? There is also a little cream to go on the top."

Ozzie was really caught between a rock and a hard place, or, as he would say, really in a 'crutch.'

Would the famous detective, Watson, pass up fresh dessert to tell his partner in crime detection some important development in the current case? Watson lost. Ozzietwo pulled out the chair on the empty side of the table and made it a foursome over apple crisp swimming in cream.

"I hope you have had your dinner? I would hate to get into trouble with your mother for spoiling yours."

Ozzietwo replied with a grin, not missing a chew, "Mubflycizin."

Mrs. Haydecker let the subject drop knowing it was just about impossible to spoil his dinner even though the probability was great that he hadn't had dinner yet.

Ozzietwo stowed away about half of his large portion of the crisp before he took a breath and decided that good manners required that he make polite dinnertime conversation. He also wanted to be invited again.

"Well, Mr. Haydecker, I hope you had a good flight and that your trip was good." Ozzietwo was at his most formal.

Mr. Haydecker, not to be outdone, answered in kind, "Yes, Oswald, thank you. It was uneventful, although I thought I might get snowed in at Stapleton in Denver. I think I missed the storm by only a couple of hours. Thank goodness I did! Have you been doing much flying lately?"

The little boy reemerged, "I flew once from Newark to Atlanta to see my grandmother. We flew at 23,000 feet." Ozzietwo spoke as if no one had ever done such a thing before. Then he lost interest in the topic and went back to demolishing the rest of the dessert.

When the last morsel had disappeared, Haydecker quickly snatched the opportunity to ask that she and Ozzietwo be excused from the table.

Ozzietwo interrupted, "I'll help, Mrs. Haydecker, carry these dishes to the kitchen for you. I can even wash and dry. I get plenty of practice." Good old Oswald was really softening up Haydecker's mother.

Mrs. Haydecker grinned in appreciation of the ploy, "Why, thank you, Ozzie. Just carrying them to the kitchen will be a great help. I don't need a human dish washer since I have an electric one that is working just fine. Both of us get out of doing the dishes."

Ozzietwo began piling up the dishes. Haydecker closed her eyes and prayed he would make it to the kitchen with the tall stack.

"Emily, you run back to the bed immediately and I will send in Ozzie just as soon as we're finished picking up here in the dining room. I know he won't be staying here long." She widened her eyes as the tilting stack of plates and cups Ozzietwo was carrying tipped alarmingly.

Haydecker settled in bed waiting for the crash of dishes. She watched the monitor trained on the foyer. There was no action there. She wished Ozzietwo would hurry up. Why did he have to be so helpful and polite, anyway? He was just looking for the next extra dessert by buttering up her mother. She had to admit it was a good tactic, though, and Ozzie was superlative at it.

Ozzietwo whipped around the corner. He moved so fast most of the time that he hardly ever huffed and puffed. Strenuous exercise was just a part of his daily routine. In fact, daily life was a strenuous proposition for Ozzietwo. Haydecker thought that at times she and Ozzie were almost like a brother and sister since neither of them had any siblings. She mused that it was kinda nice now that Ozzie2 was growing up a little.

"What's up, Watson?"

"I'm supposed to go to the Browers at seven. Mr. Brower wants me to do a chore for him." A whole stick of gum was rapidly disappearing into Ozzietwo's mouth.

"You wanna stick?" He offered Haydecker one.

The clock said "6:51."

"What does he want you to do?"

"Return his suitcase to the luggage room. He has been gone somewhere."

Haydecker was beginning to catch Ozzietwo's excitement. "Be sure you check his luggage for a sticker from Amsterdam and while you are in there be sure to poke around and see if you can find

Amsterdam on any of the other luggage or any packages in the storage room. Do you know how to spell Amsterdam?"

Ozzietwo looked thoughtful.

Spell, Oz, A M S T E R D A M"

Ozzietwo repeated after her "A S M T E D R A M."

"No, now get it right, for crying out loud! Can't you spell anything?"

Ozzietwo was getting defensive. "Spelling ain't one of my things, Haydecker, so don't get so excited. Just 'cause I can't spell doesn't mean I'm dumb. My teacher says that lots of smart people can't spell good. Good spellers are good spellers are good spellers. Period. So don't go getting your underwear all bundled!" Ozzietwo stomped his foot and clamped his mouth in a tight line.

Haydecker knew when to back off. Ozzietwo was getting pretty near the breaking point--the point where he slammed out the front door and she didn't see him again for two weeks. Usually she wanted to get rid of him and it was a good maneuver. But not today.

"OK, Oz, I'm sorry. Here let me write it down on this piece of paper and you can put it in your shirt pocket." She rammed the corner of the piece of notebook paper into the pocket of his blue and white striped polo shirt.

"Now, go, but ask Brower, kind of sneaky like, where he's been. See if you can get him to talk about his flight or the weather or something. You're good at that!"

Ozzietwo was off out the front door and disappeared around the foyer corner leaving the TV screen empty of people once more.

Haydecker hated being left behind.

The phone buzzer rang. Haydecker deliberately didn't answer. It was probably for one of her parents. She hated these cold winter school nights when all of her school friends were at home doing their homework and couldn't visit either in person or on the phone. She was missing the passing notes and giggling at the boys, especially Benjamin Harris. She really thought he was cute and every day when the TV went to the classroom she looked for him.

Ugh! Here she was, stuck playing detective games with Ozzietwo.

"Emily," her mother's voice came over the intercom, "it's for you."

"Haydecker here." She wondered who it could be at this hour.

The voice of Mad Harold boomed out at her. "Good evening, Miss Emily, this is your friendly neighborhood doorman calling to inquire after your health and well-being."

"Cut the crap, Simpson, what's new?"

"Miss Haydecker, I'm shocked at your language and your attitude. Is that any way to respond to these polite inquiries?"

Mad Harold changed gears, "Just thought I would check in with you and pass along what little news I have, but if you don't want to hear, I'll just. . ."

"Harold Simpson, cut it out this minute and tell me what is happening. I am just a little crabby tonight."

"A little!" Mad Harold laughed and continued, "Just thought that you'd want to know that Sherrie Gerot is missing, or has turned up missing, or some such thing."

"What do you mean, turned up missing?"

"What I mean is that she left for work yesterday morning and never came home last night. Her roommate, Grace Onken, finally reported it to the detectives. Something fishy is going on there. Have you seen anything up in your territory?"

"Only that Miss Onken, Grace, came to visit me for a few moments this morning. But before she could get anything about what she wanted out, we got interrupted by those two detectives and she left pretty quickly."

"Of course, what the police suspect is another murder. They have put out an APB (All Points Bulletin) and everything. Keep your eye peeled and your door locked. I am getting to like this whole business less and less. I gotta go. I'll talk to you later. You keep me posted, you hear?"

Just then, before Haydecker could sign off, a bellow erupted from the hall.

"Hold it, Simpson, we've got something going on up here. I'll let you know."

Someone in the hall, someone who sounded very much like Ozzietwo, was screaming bloody murder, "MURDER! MURDER!"

Haydecker hit the floor running and grabbed a robe as she tore out of the door.

It hadn't taken long for the screams to produce the floor's occupants. As Haydecker opened the front door and ran into the foyer, other doors were popping open, with startled and frightened residents peering out at Oswald P. McCaw II.

Ozzietwo was standing with his back to the wall facing the storage room door. His head thrown back. His eyes were shut. He was screaming. His voice was louder than Haydecker had thought possible. Ozzietwo had turned an alarming shade of grey ashes.

Haydecker ran to him and clamped her hand quickly over his mouth. Anything to get him to stop hollering.

But Ozzietwo wasn't to be stopped. He tore away from Haydecker and ran down the hall yelling some more.

Before she took out after him, Haydecker glanced through the open door of the storage room. On the floor next to a huge, black old-fashioned trunk lay a young woman. Haydecker was sure it was Sherrie Gerot. She was wearing a red coat. Her arms were bound with a rope behind her back. Her booted feet were also tied together and a gag bound her mouth tightly. She lay very still.

Ozzietwo was still running up and down the hall flapping his arms and yelling at the top of his voice. He ran smack into the broad front of Mr. Brower.

"Stop, Ozzie, stop now." He smacked Ozzietwo across the cheek, not hard enough to hurt, but hard enough to get his attention.

Ozzietwo stopped running. He stopped yelling. He sank to his knees in the corner of the hall and started to sob.

Haydecker was torn between going to comfort he friend and her curiosity about the woman lying on the Storage Room floor. She didn't enter the Storage Room but peered in for a closer look.

The hall was suddenly filled with activity. Miraculously, Ozzietwo was quiet except for taking some gasping breaths, as if he were trying to use up all the oxygen in the hall in the next five seconds.

Everyone had a comment or suggestion.

"Call the police."

"Don't touch anything."

"Is she breathing?"

"How long do you suppose she's been there?

"Where are the police, anyway? Why can't they ever be here when you need them."

"Is no one safe around here?"

Mostly everyone stood and stared while one of the residents bent over the girl. Haydecker stood with the others crowded around the entrance. She thought she could see the slow, but rhythmic rise and fall of the woman's coat front. The heavy, black buttons seemed to go up and down. But then, chiding herself, Haydecker thought it was her imagination.

"Emily, go back to the apartment immediately." Her father was pinching her arm tightly. "This is no place for you."

Haydecker thought quickly, "I gotta go get Ozzie, Dad, and then I will." She pointed to Ozzietwo down the hall and painfully wrenched her arm away from her father's grasp. She ran down to her friend who was still sitting in the corner, bent double, his head resting on his knees. He was sobbing only occasionally now.

She put her arm around him as best she could. It was awkward. She had never put her arm around Ozzie before. He had never needed an arm around him quite so much as he did now.

"Come on, Oz, let's go back to my place." She pulled him standing and grabbed his arm much like her father had manhandled her own. She whispered down to Ozzietwo as they moved by the crowd standing by the Storage Room door. "Close your eyes and don't look as we go past. Pretend it is blind man's bluff."

Just as they reached the end of the hall and had stepped into the foyer, the elevator door opened and out stepped Chubb and Sam. They were followed by Mad Harold who had obviously abandoned his door duties. He couldn't stand being out of the picture down stairs.

Mad Harold winked at Haydecker, who was glad to see a friendly face. Apparently Sam and Chubb had been more than a little bit grumpy about another body being found on the seventh floor. The detectives went directly to the crowd surrounding the storage room door.

Harold picked up Ozzietwo and put him on his shoulders, "I guess you were the hero who discovered the body? It is going to be all right now, Oz. Don't worry."

"Yeah, but Harold, I cried." Ozzietwo's voice was hushed.

"Anyone would cry, getting a scare like that. Even me and Haydecker."

Haydecker wasn't about to argue with him.

Ozzietwo was. 'Oh, yeah, Harold, I'll bet you wouldn't have cried."

"Ozzie, at the very least, I am sure I would have wet my pants; see, you didn't even wet your pants?"

"Hey, Harold, how do you know I didn't wet my pants?"

"Hey, Oz, believe me, where you are sitting, I would know if you had wet your pants! Right?"

Harold bent his head back and tried to see Ozzietwo's face.

Ozzietwo grinned a spectacular grin and clapped Harold on the head, "Right, you would sure know it by now."

Ozzietwo was feeling much better, perched up on Harold shoulders and having put some distance between himself and the scene in the Storage Room. He was feeling much safer and not quite so embarrassed. Harold had said it was OK. That made it OK with Oz. He was, after all, human.

"Let's move back from the entrance, shall we please." It was, uncharacteristically, Silent Sam trying to herd people away from the Storage Room door.

"Someone call an ambulance immediately, if one hasn't been called already. The woman is alive but not conscious."

Chubb was busy taking off the ropes and untying the gag. He immediately began to try and restore circulation in her arms and legs.

"Does anyone know this person or have any one of you seen her before?" He didn't look up as he addressed the group.

Grace Onken, who had just joined the group in the hallway, pushed forward and entered the storage room, dropping to her knees beside her friend, "She's my apartment mate, Sherrie Gerot. You remember, I phoned and reported her missing this afternoon. I'm Grace Onken. Is she going to be all right?"

"Miss, I am just the detective, not the doctor. We will be sending her to the hospital under police protection. You might like to accompany her. It is certain that she is not ready to talk yet."

Chapter XI

The detective rose to his feet, for the first time looking around at the large gathering of tenants and others crowded in the small hallway. "All right, it looks like I am going to have to interview you all again. I think we are going to have to work on the assumption that this matter is connected to the recent murder in this building. Now, who found Miss Gerot?"

He looked around, searching faces.

The hallway was silent. Finally, from up on Harold Simpson's shoulders, Ozzietwo's small voice, in contrast to his loud bellowing earlier, piped up, "I did." He gulped twice, drawing lungs full of oxygen.

"Well, suppose you come down here and tell me about it while the rest of these people go back to their apartments."

Harold lifted Ozzietwo down and set him lightly on his feet. He didn't let go of his hand, though. And Ozzietwo was just content to leave his small brown hand in Harold's huge paw.

"Now, I suppose you want your friend here to stay?"

"Two friends." Ozzietwo wanted all the help he could get. "Harold is my attorney and Haydecker is my partner. Yessir, this here's my attorney." Ozzietwo looked up at Mad Harold, small height to great height. (Ozzietwo liked the idea of having a lawyer on his team.)

Harold broke in, "That's right. I represent this esteemed gentleman and definitely wish to be present when he is questioned by the police. If you will recall, Detective, the ruling of. . ."

"All right, Simpson, all right. Don't get carried away. You'll be a pain-in-the-neck lawyer soon enough."

The detective lifted Ozzietwo to sit on the top of the trunk in the Storage Room and listened carefully while Ozzietwo told the tale of getting the key and the suitcase from Mr. Brower. He carefully described unlocking the door and flipping on the light to reveal the red-coated body, or what he had thought at the time as being a corpse covered with blood.

When Ozzietwo got to the blood part, Mad Harold had to quickly put a strong arm around his thin shoulders. Ozzietwo imagined the site again. He pointed to where he had flung the empty suitcase on his way out to yell like "bloody murder."

During this recitation, Haydecker stood very still just behind one of Mad Harold's long legs. She was hoping to escape notice and yet provide Ozzietwo with more moral support and still find out what was going on in the investigation. Either her ploy worked or Chubb knew she was there but, for some reason, was ignoring her.

"So, does Mr. Brower often ask you to do chores like this for him?"

"Heck, no, it's the first time" Ozzietwo's voice was booming out confidently now. "He says to me, he says, 'Boy, you report to my apartment directly at 7:00 because I have a chore for you to do, do you hear, now?'"

Detective Chubb couldn't help smiling at Ozzietwo's imitation of Mr. Brower's drawling voice and accent. "Did he say anything else or act suspicious?"

Ozzietwo just shook his head no.

"Okay, for now, but if you think of anything else I should know, I will probably be around the building for the rest of the evening. And while you are here, Simpson, have you seen or heard anything at your post which I ought to know about?"

"Sorry, Lieutenant, nothing to report. I didn't even know that Miss Gerot was missing until a short while ago. The building has been pretty quiet in the evening. In fact, the building has been pretty quiet all day in the last day or so."

"And, Miss Haydecker, what have you seen as you have been watching the hallways this week-end? Any sign of Miss Gerot or her abductors?"

Haydecker was really relieved that he had added that last phrase because she didn't want to confess to Chubb what she had seen in the hallway and elsewhere.

"I hadn't seen Miss Gerot in over a week. I sure haven't seen her in the hall this week."

"Well, all of you move on but this should be a warning to you to be careful until we get this thing solved." Chubb shooed them down the hall.

Harold headed for the elevator, "I had better get back on duty or old Bonomolo will be on my case. Keep me posted, Haydecker, on any developments."

Ozzietwo broke in, "Thanks, Simpson, for being my lawyer."

"Think nothing of it, Oz, when you get to be a famous running back for the Bears, you can get me tickets to all the games."

"You got it, Simpson. Seats on the 50 -yard line. Gee, do you really think I could play for the Bears?"

"I'm sure of it, Oz, you'd be the fastest thing to hit the Pro's in the Twenty-first Century."

Harold got on the elevator. Ozzie, grinning, ran up and down in place and then tore around the foyer in an imitation of broken-field running.

"Let's go back to my apartment and talk a minute before we have to go to bed." Haydecker herded Ozzietwo toward the apartment door.

Later they were settled back in Haydecker's room. Ozzietwo was perched at the end of the bed, sitting cross-legged, looking quite recovered from his bad experience. They were discussing the excitement.

"I want you to know, Airkool, that I did my detective work OK. Old Brower was in London or that's what he said when I asked him. So, is that anywhere near this Amsterdam place?"

"Ozzietwo, I don't think you have learned any geography at all at school. He might have had to fly through London from Amsterdam."

"Now, who was standing in the hall after the body was discovered?"

"Don't keep saying, 'body,' Haydecker, she wasn't dead like that other one. Even if I thought she was at first. At least there wasn't any blood. I hate blood. Yuck!"

"I got it. Close your eyes, Watson, and pretend you are on Mad Harold's shoulders again. Now picture the scene again. Who was there? Who do you see?"

Ozzietwo closed his eyes and lay backward over the end of the bed, letting his head drag on the floor while his feet were still on the top of the bed. Ozzietwo wiggled even when he was still.

"I see Mrs. Heifitz standing there with those funny things in her hair. She had no cats with her but she did have something in her hand."

"Keep going, Oz. Keep remembering. Incidentally, those things in her hair were curlers. Since you don't have to worry about curly hair, you probably wouldn't know about those.

"Don't you make fun of my hair, Haydecker. At least, it doesn't hang down in straight strings like yours."

"I am not making fun, and my hair is not entirely straight. Lots of people would love to have your curly hair and not worry about having to get permanents and stuff like that.

"Why do they call a permanent, a permanent, Haydecker, when it is sure not permanent?"

"I suppose because it is more permanent than whatever curlers do. Back to work, Ozzietwo. Think, imagine that scene. Who else do you see?"

"Of course, your dad was standing there in his jogging suit. He must not have gone running yet because he still looks chipper. Mr. Brower was there in his suit, I mean, downtown suit, after he had slapped me around." Ozzietwo raised his head up off of the floor.

"Relax, Oz, he only gave you one little slap to get you to quit bellowing. It didn't hurt you. Who else?"

"Of course, that school teacher lady was there and the General had opened the door to his apartment and was standing in the doorway with his arms crossed. He was looking mighty crabby. And Mr. Whatshisname from next to you was there but his wife wasn't. Your mom wasn't there and my mom wasn't either."

"Anybody look particularly suspicious to you in that group, Watson?"

"What do you mean. How does suspicious look, Airkool?"

"Oh, I just mean. . .I don't know what I mean. . .sneaky or doing funny stuff or something."

Ozzietwo sat up again. "Is that enough of that? I think I had better be getting home. My mother will wonder what is going on."

Ozzietwo lay back again with his head brushing the floor and then flipped off of the bed backward, landing neatly on his feet. He was off at a trot on his way to the door.

"Hey, Airkool, some night, huh? And we still don't know if anyone has been to Amsterdam." Ozzietwo left the room and then returned. "I'll tell you one thing, Haydecker, I sure ain't going to the Storage Room alone again for about five million years! See you in the morning!"

Ozzietwo raced out of the room and was a blur as he appeared briefly on the TV screen and just as quickly disappeared around the corner of the foyer. Haydecker suspected that Ozzietwo didn't want to spend too much time loitering in the hall by himself, even if he didn't know what loitering meant, he wasn't about to do it.

Haydecker looked at the clock. What had promised to be a long and boring evening had passed quickly. She went out to say goodnight to her parents.

Returning to her room, she quickly put out the light. But she just kept thinking. Who would have hit Sherrie Gerot and stashed her in the Storage Room? Or, who had lured Sherrie Gerot into the Storage Room and then knocked her out? And why? Did they mean to kill her or did they just want her out of the way?

Just as Haydecker was dropping off to sleep she heard some noises in the front of the apartment. She was awake at the click of the doorknob.

Her father and Mad Harold were standing just outside the door. Harold had Woof's leash in his hand. Haydecker turned up the volume to see if she could pick up the voices in the conversation.

Mad Harold, fortunately, was facing the camera. "Bonomolo just came in and said that Miss Gerot will be all right. She has regained consciousness but doesn't have any idea who hit her. She was trying to get into her apartment when someone bashed her from behind. She didn't see them anywhere in the hall when she was standing in front of her door. They must have come from the Storage Room and she surprised them. She didn't know anything more until she woke up in the hospital."

"She was unconscious a long while. Do you suppose they gave her a shot of something as well as hitting her over the head? Harold, I'd appreciate it, if you'd keep a special eye out on these two kids when you are in the building. I think that they think this is some kind of lark."

"Maybe they did, sir, but young Oswald had a heck of a scare tonight. He will undoubtedly be more careful and," Harold grinned, "stay out of Storage Rooms."

Haydecker switched off the set and wondered, as she drifted off again, if Ozzietwo would have nightmares tonight or, for that matter, if she would have nightmares.

Dawn and Ozzietwo showed up at about the same time the next morning. Ozzietwo's mood matched his yellow sweater and he seemed to have recovered from his scare.

"Homework done, Haydecker, although I'll bet you never did not do your homework in your whole life. Didcha?"

"Ozzietwo, go put butter in your shorts. What's it to you whether I do my homework or not. At least, I am not going to run around ignorant all my life." Haydecker was feeling a little under the weather this morning and having Ozzietwo so up-beat didn't help.

"Airkool, don't you dare have an adventure without me today."

"Got it, Watson." Haydecker thrust her thumb up in the positive sign. "You keep your eyes closed if you see any bodies lying around."

Chapter XII

Haydecker, once Ozzietwo was gone, dutifully turned on the TV and attended school for the morning. She attended but she didn't pay attention. She knew she should be minding her "P's" and "Q's" and a whole lot of other stuff. She needed to be there when Miss Gregg called on her. She didn't need a call to her parents with all the other stuff going on around here. She'd end up having to have a sitter again everyday.

The foyer and the hallway were empty pretty well all morning except for Chubb and Sam and a crew of policemen coming and going. They were still looking for possible clues in the Storage Room and talking to some residents of the building.

Haydecker was beginning to have a real struggle with her conscience over knowing that someone had been in 7A, perhaps the murderer, probably the murderer. She wished they would discover it all by themselves, quickly. If she had thought to look in the empty apartment, why hadn't they had the same idea.

She and Ozzietwo still didn't know if any of those luggage tags were from Amsterdam. Haydecker hadn't thought when she spelled Amsterdam for Ozzietwo that such luggage would probably have tags with letter codes on them such as LAX for Los Angeles and ORD for Chicago and LHR for London. It wasn't the kind of thing she could send Ozzietwo to find out.

Of course, Maeve! She had forgotten the research librarian. Because Haydecker couldn't go to the library on her own, she and Maeve would have long talks or Maeve would research special books or topics for Haydecker. But, then, again, she had to be dependent on Ozzietwo or her mother to pick up and return the materials to the library. Haydecker looked forward to the day when she could walk into the library and find Maeve and say, face-to-face, "Hi, I'm Emily Haydecker."

She punched Maeve's dial button and the automatic dialer whirred and burbled merrily about its business.

"Good afternoon, Public Library, you have reached the research and information desk. Maeve Powell speaking."

"Hi, Miss Powell, this is Emily."

"Emily," Maeve's voice sounded glad to hear her. "What a long time it has been since I've heard from you. I thought maybe you had been allowed to go back to school. I thought I had been utterly forsaken."

"No such luck yet, Maeve, I mean about going back to school, but when I do get to go out again, I will be coming to the library to do my own research. You can count on it." It seemed as though Haydecker had known Maeve Powell forever and yet they had never seen each other.

"I'll look forward to it, Emily, perhaps I can even take a break and we'll go down to the library cafeteria and have a soda, my treat, of course, to celebrate your recovery.

"Now, what can I do for you today? Business has been a little slow the past few days so I hope you have a real hard problem to research."

"Not so hard, Miss Powell." Haydecker explained what she wanted to know but not why she wanted to know it.

"Do you want to hold, Emily, or shall I call you back?"

"Find it when you have time this afternoon and call me back. I won't be going any place."

"You'll hear from me in a little while, then." Miss Powell rang off.

Emily Marie Haydecker stared at the empty foyer and was bored. She was lost in a thousand thoughts, so lost, in fact, that the appearance of Dwight Mohr in the foyer nearly escaped her attention. He stood in the very center so he could see in all directions, down the long arm of the hall and over to the edge of the foyer where the elevators were located.

He stood there casually, as if it were the most usual thing in the world to hang around outside your own apartment. He lit a cigarette even though the signs in the lobbies and foyers of the whole building definitely discouraged smoking. He leaned against the wall next to the rubber plant and flicked his ashes in the general direction of the huge leaves.

A door opened down the hall where Haydecker couldn't see. Dwight Mohr suddenly started pacing the floor and looking at his wristwatch. Golda Heifitz came into view, carefully pulling on her gloves.

"Good afternoon, Mrs. Heifitz, and how are you this afternoon. This is certainly a perturbing state of affairs we have on this floor this week, isn't it?" Dwight Mohr surely knew how to draw attention away from himself.

Mrs. Heifitz started in, gripping her handbag tightly against her body, "And isn't it something else. A body is not safe, simply not safe, what with murders and hijackings and coshings. I always felt safe in this building but I was saying to Clothilde just this morning that I may, indeed, start looking for some place safer. Goodness knows we pay enough so that they ought to assign a body guard to each person in the building."

"I am sure the police are doing everything they can to get to the bottom of the matter. They have some extra personnel assigned to the building. I am sure that it wouldn't hurt, though, to take extra precautions and not go loitering about the halls."

Haydecker though she saw a half a smile play across Dwight's face as he turned away from Mrs. Heifitz.

She hugged her ample handbag to her even more ample bosom. "Why, it could be anyone doing these crimes. Even someone on this floor. Why, it could even be you, couldn't it, Mr. Mohr. You could be. . ." Golda Heifitz stopped in mid-sentence, backed up and then made her way to the elevator where she jabbed at the DOWN button.

Dwight Mohr was not content to let the conversation drop. "You are right, Mrs. Heifitz, it could be any one of us. Mr. Brower, the General, Grace Onken, even, it could be you!"

Mrs. Heifitz looked so stunned at the suggestion that she let the elevator door open and close while she stood there with her mouth agape.

"Oh no, Mr. Mohr, not hardly could I get up the strength to strangle someone or smush them on the top of the head. Oh no, Mr. Mohr, surely we are looking for a big, strong able person, not a weak old lady." She punched the elevator button again.

"Don't underestimate the strength of women. It just might be one of you."

Golda Heifitz was considerably steamed by this time as the elevator door finally opened again. This time she collected herself sufficiently to get on.

"No, oh no, Mr. Mohr, I am sure you are quite wrong. You are probably saying that only to divert attention away from yourself." The elevator door closed on a wide-eyed Golda Heifitz staring at Dwight Mohr across the lobby. It had suddenly occurred to her that she might be right.

Dwight Mohr threw back has head and laughed at the closed elevator door. The spell of merriment was only momentary as he glanced at his watch again and frowned. He lit another cigarette and resumed his pacing.

Finally, with a look at the empty hall, he stomped over to the elevator and pushed the button. Almost immediately the light went on, the bell pinged and the door opened. Dwight Mohr got on the elevator standing exactly in the center of the front. With his hands clasped behind his back, he rocked back and forth on his heels as he waited for the door to close. And then, the foyer was empty and Haydecker was left wondering who the mystery person was who had missed the meeting with DD Mohr.

But Haydecker did not have to wonder long. Two persons appeared in the foyer. The sound of the door opening and closing down the long arm of the hall produced Oswald McCaw striding into the foyer. He carried a newspaper under his arm and he stood momentarily in the center of the foyer. At first, he started toward the elevator, then he paused and turned abruptly and strode toward the Haydecker's door.

But, he stopped just as quickly again when the elevator door opened and Grace Onken got off to stand facing him. For a minute no one said anything. Oswald McCaw looked hesitant and Grace Onken looked scared.

Haydecker was suddenly inclined to agree that the whole business was getting to everyone. Nobody she had seen today wasn't jumpy.

"Good afternoon, Miss Onken." Oswald McCaw spoke a he moved toward her.

"Good afternoon, Mr. McCaw." Grace backed away with every pace that he took toward her. Her eyes got wider and wider.

Suddenly, McCaw stepped around her to reach the elevator button. She flinched before she realized he was just summoning the elevator.

A look of relief washed over her face.

"I do hope that Miss Gerot is recovering from her unfortunate ordeal. What does she say about it?" Mr. McCaw inquired politely about Grace's roommate.

"I've just come from the hospital where she'll have to stay at least for another day for observation. She is recovering nicely; the doctors think that there won't be any permanent damage."

"Good, good, it sounds like an excellent outcome to a deplorable situation."

The elevator doors closed and swept all sight of Mr. McCaw away and Grace hesitated in the middle of the foyer. She looked around to see who was there and then she tore off down the hall. Haydecker heard the rattle of her keys in the lock and then a loud slam.

Haydecker was left to speculate. Was DD Mohr waiting for Grace Onken or Oswald McCaw or, perhaps, for person or persons unknown.

The telephone interrupted her thoughts. "May I please speak to Miss Haydecker. This is Maeve Powell calling."

"Hi, Miss Powell, Haydecker here."

"Hello, again, Emily. Here is the information you wanted." She proceeded to relay the call letters for the cities Haydecker had requested. "By the way, are the police making any headway on the unfortunate occurrences in your apartment building? We are all a little nervous about it happening in our area of town."

"If you are nervous there, Miss Powell, you can imagine what everyone is here."

"Well, do be careful Emily, and I hope the information is what you needed and you can get a good grade on the assignment." Haydecker would tell that Miss Powell was really fishing for information as to why she wanted the call letters for the cities. Haydecker had to admit to herself that it was a strange request and that she couldn't think of any reasonable explanation to cover her request.

"It will really help with the assignment, Miss Powell, and thanks again." Haydecker blushed at the lie when she hung up the phone.

The clock continued to creep along, minute by minute, through the day. Haydecker knew that she was really waiting for Ozzietwo to come home from school. What a turn around that was when she used to dread having him pester her every day when he brought her school papers and books.

Just as the clock clicked 3:57, her mother came into the room. She was dressed in her coat to go out. "Emily, I just must go to the store for a few groceries. It is more important than ever that you keep the door locked and don't let anyone but Ozzie or your father in."

"I'll be all right, Mom, Ozzie will be here any minute to keep me company and bring my homework."

"I've left a plate of cookies on the counter and have poured glasses of milk which are in the fridge. Ozzie can get them for both of you. Now take care. I don't mean to alarm you but I do want you to be more careful until the matter is resolved."

She went out the front door, turning and clicking the lock before she walked toward the elevator. Before she could reach the DOWN button, the door opened and, in a blur of motion, Ozzietwo plunged across the foyer, nearly toppling Haydecker's mother.

"Sorry, Mrs. Haydecker, I didn't mean to nearly mash you. I guess I just wasn't watching where I was going."

"Hi, Ozzie, I'm going out for a few minutes. I was hoping you would be along to keep Emily company while I am gone."

"Sure, Mrs. Haydecker, I was fixing to see her anyway." He tore over to the Haydecker's door. "Let me in, Haydecker." He turned to make sure that Mrs. Haydecker was on the elevator and then he added, "Airkool, open up!"

Ozzietwo came through the bedroom, peeling off his backpack bag and his parka. He scattered the books and papers over the bed, sorting those that were for Haydecker and those that were his own. It took some sorting, not because there were so many papers, but because Ozzietwo's filing system was no system at all.

"So, how did it go today, Watson? Any news from the institution?"

"They had about eleven million questions about what is going on at the Towers. Not that I can blame them. The teachers got pretty mad because the kids wanted to hear all about it instead of listening to them."

"Go get some cookies in the kitchen; the milk is in the fridge. Then, we'll decide where to go from here."

Ozzietwo whizzed out of the room and Haydecker glanced up at the TV screen. The elevator light had just popped on. Haydecker waited to see who would get off this time. The seventh floor had been like a bus station today.

An old lady got off. She was thin and stooped over and dressed in a long coat. She had a veil which was pulled down, hiding the whole top part of her face. Her whole head was twisted slightly to one side. Haydecker couldn't remember having seen her on the seventh floor before. She certainly didn't look like one of Mrs. Heifitz sisters dressed like that.

Ozzietwo came into the room. The plate of cookies perched precariously on top of one of the milk glasses. He looked up at the TV screen. Who's that old lady?"

"Ozzietwo, don't look at anything until you put those cookies and milk down," she yelled, grabbing the plate and delivering it safely to the bedside table.

Ozzietwo crammed a cookie into his mouth and looked up again. "What's she doing? I sure haven't seen her before. She is probably one of old Goldy's sisters. She got a ton of them, you know."

"They don't come over here very often. I am really surprised that one of them has visited today when I know that Golda went out somewhere earlier this afternoon. I am pretty sure she hasn't come back yet, at least, I haven't seen her."

"Maybe it is the General's girlfriend." Ozzietwo hooted with laughter. "She really looks like his type, ugly and ornery." Ozzietwo was spilling cookies crumbs all over in his amusement at himself.

"I wish she'd do something beside just stand there. What is she waiting for?" Ozzietwo had quit chewing and was just staring at the TV screen with his jaw hanging loose.

The old lady continued to stand just a few paces away from the elevator and was looking from left to right but not looking like she was going to leave that particular spot.

"Do you suppose something is wrong with her and we should go and help?"

Ozzietwo, even though he wasn't a Boy Scout, did his part, mostly when it came to helping old ladies. Of course, it helped if they baked cakes and cookies.

"Aw, Haydecker, where have you ever seen such big feet on an old lady? They must be 16D's, at least. Haydecker, promise me that when you get to be an old lady you won't wear shoes like that!" Haydecker stared at the TV and then she turned to stare at the small body stuffing cookies into its mouth.

"Ozzietwo, those feet don't belong to an old lady. I'll bet my chemistry set. Watson, Watson, I think that it is someone in disguise."

Again, Ozzietwo stopped chewing; he eased down on the side of the bed closest to the TV set. His eyes were wide. Haydecker sat behind him. Neither of them spoke as they watched the old woman clumsily pull off one white glove and fumble at the clasp of her handbag.

"What do we do now, Airkool?" Ozzietwo's voice wasn't much more than a whisper even though there was no danger that he would be heard in the hall. "I'll run out there and tackle the old bag and knock him cold.

Haydecker grabbed him, just in time. The yellow sweater stretched when she had a hold on him in the back. "You'll do no such thing. You would think that last night would have taught you that this is nothing to be foolish about. As tough as you are, that person is a lot bigger and a whole lot meaner. Do you realize that that person might have murdered someone or knocked someone silly and tied them up?"

"Well, Haydecker, we've got to do something."

"I'll call downstairs and maybe Mr. Bonomolo or Mad Harold are around and can call the police or come up or something."

Haydecker grabbed the phone, but before she could reach for the numbers, the elevator door opened to reveal Mrs. Brower and Marcia with their arms full of parcels. The old lady/man took one look at the mother and daughter and quickly closed his handbag. With quickness and agility which gave lie to the idea of an old lady, he darted into the stairwell. The two women paid no attention and continued their conversation as they walked down the hall.

"Shall we go out and look down the stairwell?" It was a brave sounding Ozzietwo again. "She's so. . .he's so slow in those shoes we'd catch him in a minute."

"And then, what would we do, Ozzietwo? Just what would you do if you caught up with him? No way are we going to end up like Sherrie Gerot on the floor of the Storage Room. For a change, we will do what we should have done when we found the key. We'll call Chubb and Sam."

"Aw, Haydecker, does that mean we can't detect any more?"

"Relax, Oz, we'll just tell them about the old lady. We don't have to tell everything we know."

Haydecker grinned at Ozzietwo. "Let's call and then we will practice what we are going to say. No way am I going to give up detecting at this late date. We are in too deep."

Hercule Poirot's loyal and competent assistant, Watson, grinned an ear-splitter. But Haydecker wasn't grinning. How was she going to talk her way out of this mess?

Chapter XIII

Chubb and Sam were at the police station when Haydecker put in the call. "This is Emily Haydecker. I just thought I ought to report that Oswald Macaw II and I spotted an unknown and suspicious person in the seventh floor lobby a few moments ago."

Ozzietwo stuck out his tongue at Haydecker when she used his given name.

"Was it the man in the black coat?" Chubb's voice came clearly over the wire.

"We're pretty sure that it was a man disguised as woman."

"What gives you that idea?" Chubb was immediately skeptical. "How do you mean, man disguised as a woman?"

"The woman had feet the size of tugboats and moved like a rabbit. It didn't look like any old lady I ever saw on either side of a circus tent."

There was a momentary silence on the other end of the line. Then Chubb's voice came back on the line, "We'll be right over. Call down stairs and see if Harold Simpson is in the building. Have him come right up if he's there." The line went dead

Haydecker was made a little nervous by Chubb's tone and she wasted no time in punching Harold's redial button. "Tower's Lobby, Simpson speaking."

Haydecker was relieved to hear his voice. "Seen anybody suspicious, Harold?"

"Zat you, Haydecker? What do you mean by suspicious?" She could tell that Mad Harold was immediately alert.

"Like a little old lady in a long black coat who's really a man clumping around in size 50 wedgies."

Ozzietwo piped up from behind, "Yeah, just the kind of shoes Haydecker wants when she goes back to school."

"Shut up, Oswald."

To Mad Harold Haydecker continued, "The police said you are supposed to come up until they can get here."

"I'll be there pronto," Mad Harold sounded serious, "I guess I'll take the stairway. I'll see you in a minute or two."

"Be careful, Harold, over and out."

"Shall we meet him half-way on the stairs?" Ozzietwo was bouncing on the bed, his fingers making the once small hole in his red sweater larger and larger.

"So help me, Ozzietwo, if you so much as make a move to leave this room until Harold comes, I'll clobber you into next week!"

"Aw, Haydecker, you have no spirit of adventure!"

"Well, I'd have to agree that Sherrie Gerot is probably really having an adventure in the hospital right now." Haydecker's mouth was stretched in a straight line and Ozzietwo's eyes were like full moons on dark nights!

As they waited and watched the TV picture of the hall, Hercule Poirot and Watson remained motionless until M. Poirot put his arm around the shoulders of his colleague in the detection of crime. They waited. Still Mad Harold didn't come through the door.

Suddenly Haydecker jumped off the bed. Ozzietwo jumped off too although he didn't know why, except that jumping off felt better than sitting still.

"I don't know about you," Haydecker's voice shook, "but I just can't sit here and wait. I am going to put some jeans on and, if he doesn't show pretty quick, we are gonna take a look in that stairwell. After all, it is my fault he started up the stairwell."

"But, Haydecker, they told you to tell him to do it," Ozzietwo's voice had risen about two octaves and some beads of perspiration stood out around his hairline and on his upper lip.

"Keep your eyes on the screen, Oz, I'll only be a minute." She dove into the closet and emerged almost immediately with the sweatshirt and jeans and tennies she didn't wear often enough these days. She disappeared into the dressing room off the bathroom. Noises were especially loud: the sniffing of Woof's breathing, the faint crackling of the audio on the TV set, the soft rustling of Haydecker's flannel robe and pajamas being discarded and a very faint squeak as Ozzie bounced nervously on the bed. Ozzietwo thought that he had never heard anything so loud as all the silence.

"Hold your horses, Oz, I'm coming."

"I can hold the horses, but I can't hold everything else. With a huge bounce, Ozzietwo went up in the air and his feet hit the floor just churning. "I forgot to go to the bathroom earlier. I'll use your folks, Haydecker, cause I gotta go quick."

He tore from the room just as Haydecker emerged from the dressing room. "Good grief, Ozzietwo, you always wait too long.

Don't pee on the seat. It makes my mother furious." She grinned as she sat down to put on her tennis shoes. It was a good thing that Ozzietwo was wearing his.

He came back into the room just as she was finishing combing her hair. No matter how much Ozzietwo tore around, he never seemed to be short of breath. It must be because he was in terrific shape from living life perpetually on the run. Haydecker was even more conscious of it because her breath was so short after just walking down the hall and she was continually tired. She had to get better soon.

They went out into the hall together making sure that the door was secured and that Haydecker had her key. She didn't want to be stuck in the foyer with the lady in the wedgies and no key to get back into the apartment.

"Well, what shall we do, Haydecker? Try the elevator or try the stairs?" They just stood there and looked at each other.

Ozzietwo swallowed, "I got it," his voice was kind of high and thin, "let's go and yell real loud down the stairwell and see if he answers."

Haydecker nodded. She knew Ozzietwo was up to that! They went over to the stair door. Haydecker was first and ever so slowly and carefully, an inch at a time, pushed the door open. They listened.

"Geez, Haydecker, I don't hear anything, at least, I don't hear anything but you huffing and puffing. Shall I holler?"

Haydecker nodded in agreement.

Ozzietwo took a huge breath, "Hey, Simpson, you down there?"

They listened again. Nothing, but then something.

Haydecker held her breath. Ozzietwo's eyes widened as his mouth dropped open. His voice shook, "Did you hear something, Haydecker?"

"I think so," her voice was but a whisper. "Do it again, Oz."

"Hey, Simpson, zat you?"

Again, louder, this time, there was an unmistakable noise in the stairwell but nothing that could be counted as words.

"Suppose it isn't him, Haydecker. Suppose it is somebody who is trying to trap us into coming into the stairwell?"

"Yeah, but suppose it is him and that every minute counts and that he is bleeding to death and we could save him."

"But. . .but. . .what good does it do us if we end up in the same shape." Ozzietwo, without thinking, scratched where his pants pinched.

The moment of indecision went on and on. Finally, Haydecker said firmly, "You hold the door open and I will lean over and peek and see if I can see anything."

Ozzietwo swung the door all the way back to assure himself that no one was behind it. Ever so carefully Haydecker walked to the edge and peered over the railing. Ozzietwo leaned against the open door with his eyes closed.

"I can't see anything from up here," Haydecker's voice was muffled as she leaned over the railing. Her knuckles were white from gripping the iron bar.

So intent were both Haydecker and Ozzietwo on their little drama in the stairway that they did not notice the rumble of the elevator cables through the wall right next to the stairwell. The "bang" of the elevator bell nearly pitched Haydecker over the rail and threw Ozzietwo back into the foyer as the heavy door started to swing closed.

"Good grief, Haydecker, it is a good thing that I went to the bathroom before we came out here. Who do you suppose it is?"

"I hope it is the detectives. Quick, get back into the foyer."

The elevator door opened and once again Chubb and Sam stood staring at the seventh floor foyer of The Towers.

"Well, where's Simpson?" Chub growled.

Haydecker almost hated to tell him. "I don't know. He hasn't shown up yet. We think he might be down here where we just heard a noise."

"You kids have great big imaginations, that's what! I'll have a look." He started down the steps and got to the first landing.

"Oh, good grief, call the ambulance. We've got another one." Haydecker and Ozzietwo and Sam all rushed for the stairwell.

Chubb was first down the stairs, moving lightly in spite of his size. He knelt beside Mad Harold. Ozzietwo and Haydecker followed, although they both slowed down the last step or two. Sam was on his cell.

Simpson lay on the cement floor of the 6th floor landing. His face was a pale white and a blood stain was seeping onto the grey floor from under his head.

"Simpson, Simpson, can you hear me?" Chubb was calm. Haydecker thought that he probably saw bashed heads every day.

"We thought we heard him making a noise a few minutes ago but we didn't know if we should go and look or not." Haydecker's voice was thin and quivery. Her face was almost as pale as Mad Harold's. Even Ozzietwo's normally dark brown satin skin had turned an ashy grey color.

Chubb felt the carotid artery. He cleared his throat, "That's good! His pulse is strong. He must have just gotten a good bash on the head. But, we must be careful not to move him before the medics get here."

Haydecker was anxiously bending toward the doorman's face. Ozzietwo was half over and half around her shoulder. He had slipped his hand into Haydecker's.

Suddenly, Harold's eyes flew open. Ozzietwo yipped and jumped four feet up and two feet back. "He's alive!" Ozzietwo closed his eyes and sat back against the cement block wall. Haydecker grinned at Mad Harold. He tried to grin back.

"Hey, Haydecker, what's up? Did you bash me from behind?" His voice was as weak as his grin. "I wouldn't put it past you."

"You know, Simpson, I know better than to bash you on the head because your head is too hard to have it cause any damage. I would be afraid that what little brains you have would leak out."

Ozzietwo was still sitting against the wall doing some pretty heavy breathing.

"Hey, Ozzietwo, Simpson is going to make it. Lighten up!" Ozzietwo made no move to get up.

Haydecker sat down on the cold cement floor beside Harold to wait until the ambulance crew arrived to take him to the hospital.

"What happened, Harold? Did you see anything?"

Harold groaned and closed his eyes. "Not a thing. I was rushing up the stairs two and three at a time, because I thought it would be faster and because I thought that if there were anyone in the stairwell, I would be able to surprise them."

"Instead, you got surprised!" Haydecker chimed in.

"I guess. Tell Chubb that I didn't see anything of my attacker except a flash of stars when I got hit and then everything went black. What was it anyway? A ton of bricks?"

"Whatever it was, they didn't leave a weapon around. Maybe the doctors will be able to tell. If it was that old lady person that Ozzie and I saw in the hallway, she could have hit you with his purse."

"Decide, Haydecker, whether it was a him or a her."

"You got me, Simpson, I haven't any idea and neither does Ozzie. To us it looked like a little of each. I haven't seen very many ladies in my time with shoes the size of those puppies."

Suddenly, a face peered over the stair railing. "The body down here?"

"It isn't a body," Haydecker called back defensively. She reminded herself of Ozzietwo. "It's a person who is wounded. Now get down here fast."

Two white-coated attendants clattered down the stairs with a mobile stretcher. They spent considerable time trying to maneuver in the narrow space of the stair landing.

"Lady," one of them said, "It would be better if you and the kid would go on upstairs now so that we can load him up."

Haydecker looked around to see who the attendant was talking to. With a half-smile she grabbed Ozzietwo's hand and pulled him up the steps. She called to Harold over her shoulder, "Hang tough, Simpson, we'll see you top side."

In the foyer on the 7th floor, there were more strange men, both dressed in police uniforms and in business suits. They were banging on doors and talking with residents as the doors were answered.

When Haydecker and Ozzietwo appeared in the hall, Sam came right over. "Well, how is Simpson doing? Do you think he will be able to answer a few questions before they cart him off to the white house?"

"I think he is going to make it. Ask him if he can answer questions." Haydecker thought that was the first time she had heard Silent Sam put two sentences together.

"I also think it is time that we had a talk again. You two kids to seem to keep ending up in the middle of this. Let's go back to your apartment and get out of this mess and will talk a little. We will talk to Simpson at the hospital."

Haydecker let them into the apartment. Silent Sam went directly for her bedroom where he could see the TV monitor. "OK, let's have it. What happened and what did you see?

Haydecker let Ozzietwo talk a little bit and tell what there was to tell and about how they had spotted the strange person in the foyer. Haydecker was interested in watching the proceedings in the foyer and hall. She was interested to note who had been home that afternoon since the detectives were bringing out the residents to sit in the foyer and be interrogated.

"Hey, there's my mom." It was a rare appearance by Ozzietwo's mother who did not frequently leave her apartment. Haydecker thought she looked tired, but then decided that living with Ozzietwo would make anyone look tired. "I think I'll go out and see her for a minute." Ozzietwo was gone!

In the foyer, Ozzietwo grabbed his mother's arm and the two hurried back to their apartment. Mrs. McCaw's appearance was followed by Golda, this time with a cat under each arm. Then came Mrs. Brower but daughter, Marcia, was nowhere to be seen. Finally, General Cargill sat in the chair designated for the questionees. He was dressed, as usual, in a shirt, tie and coat. (Haydecker idly wondered if he went to bed dressed like that.)

"I sure would like to figure out what is going on around here." It was Silent Sam talking, almost to himself.

Haydecker was listening carefully. "You mean, why all this stuff is going on on seventh floor of this building?"

"Sure, what is so special about this place that we keep having these incidents. To be sure, the murder of that lady we found, had something to do with some operation. We are checking into the background of everyone on this floor, you can be sure."

"Oh, and who looks suspicious."

"Listen, young lady, there are some things you don't have to know."

Haydecker said, being smart, "Sure, but you want to know everything that I know."

"We'll let me assure you that you and young McCaw are not under suspicion for murder. But sometimes I have the feeling that there may be some other stuff you know. Tell me, Miss Haydecker, what it is, Emily? Tell me, Emily, if you were the detective in this case, who would you look more closely at?"

Haydecker, tried to look her most important and tried not to look guilty of about eight crimes, one of which was suppression of evidence from the investigating authorities.

"Well, I could be pretty sure that Golda wasn't involved, and my parents, and Ozzietwo's mother and probably not the Brower ladies and the General is too old, isn't he, to be doing any stuff like that? That narrows things down a little, doesn't it. The second thing I would do is to search every square inch of the seventh floor."

Silent Sam looked at her strangely and without so much as a snort got up from his chair and started toward the door.

"Young lady, keep your door locked at all times. And that is an order! And see if you can keep young McCaw corralled a little bit. What ever you do don't let him run around alone. Or you for that matter, either." He strode out of the room and out of the apartment.

Ozzietwo had reappeared in the foyer and was inching toward the door of 7C. When he saw Silent Sam emerge, he darted in behind his back.

The chaos in the hall had calmed down. Silent Sam went directly to Chubb and they had a conference. In a low voice, that Haydecker could not hear, Chubb called two uniformed cops over to him. They conferred and then the two in uniform went off down the hall.

Silent Sam got on the elevator and the door closed behind him. Chubb squared his shoulders and started toward Haydecker's door.

He stood directly in front of the door and faced the television camera.

During this whole silent scene, for a change, maybe for the first time in his life, Oswald MaCaw II was quiet, was so quiet, in fact, that Haydecker had to look at him to be sure that he was really breathing. Haydecker wonder if he, too, was thinking what in the world was going to happen next.

Chapter XIV

"Miss Haydecker, Miss Haydecker, can you hear me? Please let me in so that we can continue our interview." Haydecker suddenly realized that Chubb must have been talking to her while she was gathering wool. She pressed the buzzer quickly.

Ozzietwo looked up at her quickly. "Are we gonna tell, Haydecker?"

"Tell what, Ozzie?"

"Oh, I donno, all the stuff we know that they don't!"

"Just wait and see how much we know that they don't."

Chubb came into the room and as usual plumped down on his favorite chair so that he could see the coming and going in the foyer. He seemed relaxed and didn't say anything for a few minutes. Haydecker wondered if he was going to try and wait them out. She could feel Ozzietwo kicking the edge of the bed with his heels.

Haydecker decided to break the conversational ice jam. "So, how is Miss Gerot? Has she been released from the hospital?"

"She will be released this afternoon. Unfortunately, she could tell us nothing. Whoever attacked her came up from behind and she never saw a thing. Let me ask you something. How long have you known Harold Simpson?"

"Harold Simpson!" Haydecker was stunned. "Harold Simpson! You mean Mad Harold?" She couldn't imagine that there would be any serious question on the part of the police about Mad Harold.

"Don't get alarmed. It is my business to be curious about everyone who had been in the building and especially who had spent much time on this floor. I just wondered what you knew about him."

Oh, I guess, I have known him just about ever since I can remember. He started working here while he was in college when the building opened. And then he graduated from college and has been in law school for a year. He has been here quite a while. Why, what's he done suspicious? To tell you the truth I don't think Mad Harold could kill a lady bug. Besides he is just about the smartest person I have ever met. I think he is too smart to have done this stuff, especially attacking himself." Haydecker giggled. She was getting a little nervous.

"I don't mean to imply that whoever was doing this was acting alone. We have reason to believe that the criminals are a couple of people acting together. One of them lives here or works here and the other one is the person in disguise who is in and out of the building."

"Well," Haydecker shifted her weight and humphed, "I surely don't think it is Mad Harold. Well...he is ...well...one of our best friends. He really helps Oz and me a lot."

"And what do you say, young man?" Chubb addressed the question to Ozzietwo this time.

"I agree with Haydecker. He wouldn't hurt a flea. At least, no flea that I have ever met. Heck, you might as well suspect Mr. Bonomolo at that rate. I suspect him more than I would Harold Simpson."

"And why do you suspect him?" Chubb jumped right in.

Haydecker was quick to assist Ozzietwo. "He didn't say he DID suspect him, he just said you might was well. There is a difference."

"Sorry," Chubb seemed sufficiently contrite.

"Sure, well, Mr. Bonomolo is not gonna murder people in his own building and take all the heat and get into all that trouble, is he?" It was Ozzie who piped up. His squeaky voice sounded strangely unused.

"Well, you never know, young man. When money is involved, lots of it, people will do quite a number of things." Chubb answered thoughtfully.

"Money?" Haydecker perked up at the thought. "How do you know that there is money involved in this and that the motive is not revenge or passion or something else?"

"To tell the truth, Miss Haydecker, we don't know for sure, but the method of the murder plus the fact that we have been unable to connect the dead girl with anyone indicates that she was probably not well known to anyone here, including her murderer. But most important, the attacks have continued, first Miss Gerot and now Simpson. They seem an unlikely trio to have something in common like being the objects of passion or blackmail."

There was a lot of coming and going in the hall with both plain clothes detectives and uniformed policemen wandering about. They were searching, again, every square inch of the hall.

The elevator bell went off and the door opened to reveal one of the objects of their previous conversation. Tony Bonomolo stood just inside the foyer talking and gesticulating furiously. Without being able to hear his words, Haydecker wanted to laugh. She glanced at Chubb. He seemed to have a slight smirk beginning around his mouth.

"It looks like Mr. Bonomolo would like to have a little conversation. I guess I had better get out there and take the heat off of the other officers or I will never hear the end of it.

"It seems that we can never get this little discussion finished. I think that there are still probably some things that we might like to talk about." He grinned at Haydecker and Ozzietwo.

Haydecker didn't grin back.

"If Mr. Bonomolo brought the keys, we are going into that empty apartment across the hall. As a matter of fact, even if Mr. Bonomolo didn't bring the keys, we are going into the apartment across the hall. I can't imagine how I missed that in the first place. In that flurry of interviews after the first murder, it never occurred to investigate that apartment since there was no name on the list for it."

Haydecker and Ozzietwo sat still.

"There isn't any possibility that the two of you would like to come along, is there?"

Haydecker couldn't believe that he was asking. She glanced at Ozzietwo as he turned to stare at her. His mouth fell open. Haydecker didn't see how they could refuse.

"Well, sure, I suppose so." She wanted to say that all he had told them so far was that they should stay out of things and now he was inviting them to get into things.

The three of them emerged from the Haydecker's' door. Mr. Bonomolo was warmed up and started bemoaning to Chubb the dire consequences that all this was going to have on the building, on the owner, but most of all on him personally.

"Relax, Mr. Bonomolo, we will get this cleared up. Certainly you are not responsible for what has been happening. I have assured the owners that your management has been effective and efficient. You have nothing to worry about, unless you were the one committing the crimes."

"What!" Mr. Bonomolo started to explain again but Chubb just took him by the arm and steered him toward the door of Apartment 7A.

"Incidentally, I have to use the master key, because the regular apartment key is missing from the key board."

"Who has access to these keys?"

"Well, they're in my office which is locked when I am not in it." Mr. Bonomolo turned the key in 7A.

"Always locked?" Chubb questioned.

"Well, mostly." Bonomolo gave Chubb a reluctant shrug of his well-padded shoulders.

The apartment was cold just like it had been when Haydecker had first been in it. It looked empty, very empty. It was cold, very, very cold. Haydecker's first reaction was to look around and see if she could see any tell-tale signs of those persons who had been in the apartment, either the supposed criminals or herself. It was as she remembered it in the kitchen and the living room. She would have given anything to be able to get another look in that drawer of the refrigerator.

"Why are you keeping it so cold in here. Aren't you afraid the pipes in the kitchen and the bathroom will freeze? And, it certainly can't be very easy on the heating bills?" Chubb questioned Mr. Bonomolo.

"Cold!" Tony Bonomolo nearly shrieked. "I didn't know it was so cold in here."

"In other words, it has been sometime since you inspected the apartment?"

"With all the excitement I guess I have missed a few days. I didn't think it would hurt anything and I was just too busy."

Suddenly Chubb turned and looked down into the up turned faces of Ozzietwo and Haydecker. Their surprise caused them to jump back, almost in unison. "And when were the two of you in here, and what did you find?"

Haydecker was caught off guard. She stammered and it happened so quickly that she couldn't deny anything.

She felt a flood a relief. At last she was going to have to tell the little secrets that she and Ozzietwo had been keeping.

Ozzietwo's eyes were as big as O's and he made a funny noise as he drew in his breath. Haydecker mumbled in a whisper to him as the other men went on through the apartment.

"Don't worry, Oz. It is better this way. Maybe we can even get them not to tell our parents if we are careful and come clean. I hope like everything that we can convince them. I will really be in deep doo doo, if they feel like they gotta tell and we have to go to jail or something."

"Oh, no, Haydecker, you don't really think they will?" Ozzietwo grabbed her arm.

The bedroom was empty. Haydecker peered into the closet. It was empty too. Chubb eyed her strangely. He seemed to know more than she thought he did. You could never be too careful of these detectives. But, then, maybe that is why they were detectives, because they found out stuff, stuff that most people didn't notice. They found out stuff that children found out because the children nosed around and got into business that didn't concern them and then failed to tell their parents or the police when they should have.

Haydecker could see that they had a bad patch ahead of them or rather that she had a bad patch ahead. Oz would squeak through OK. He wouldn't get into so much trouble because he was the youngest. But they would all look at her as responsible.

"You ready for a little chat, Miss Haydecker, Mr. McCaw?" Chubb's voice was excessively polite. "Perhaps we could go to the Haydecker apartment again. It is really helpful to have the TV monitor to keep an eye on as we talk."

Chubb went out the door of the empty apartment first. He was followed by Haydecker. Ozzietwo brought up the rear. The party did not move very fast. However, the first marcher in the party was more enthusiastic than the last two. The rear of the column was decidedly dispirited.

Chubb settled himself in his usual chair in Haydecker's room. Haydecker climbed into bed, suddenly very tired from all the excitement. Ozzietwo sat on the edge of the bed. His heels went clunk, clunk in a rhythmic pattern as he banged them against the wood of the bed frame.

Chubb looked at them expectantly. "Well, where do we begin?"

While Haydecker knew she couldn't tell him, she also knew good and well that she would have to go back to that empty apartment again.

Chapter XV

And so, Haydecker began the story with Ozzietwo chiming in whenever he had something to add. Occasionally he would erupt in surprise when he heard something that Haydecker had forgotten to tell him before. And then, only for a few seconds he would pout and remain silent.

"OK, so, Oz, maybe I forgot to tell you a few things. Don't get your nose so out of shape. The important thing is that we fill in the detectives here. This has gone too far."

Ozzietwo bounced up and down on the bed in agreement.

Haydecker had described her visits to the empty apartment and she and Ozzietwo had turned over the key. The one thing she had not told the detective was that she had told someone that she knew his identity. She was sure that Chubb's knowledge of that would necessitate putting a guard on the apartment for 24 hours a day. And, in turn, her mother and father would have to be told. The last thing in the world she wanted was to have them know that she had violated the trust that they had placed in leaving her alone in the apartment. She was sure that her mother suspected as much already.

"OK, Miss Haydecker, anything else that seems to have slipped your mind in the past few days? Anything else that you neglected to report to your friendly police detectives?"

"I can't think of anything just now, but I will certainly call if I can think of anything."

"You just make sure you do that, young lady. No more wandering around in empty apartments alone."

"Definitely not. It was too cold and made my legs ache."

"Cold?" Chubb repeated the word quizzically.

"Don't you remember that I told you that each time in the apartment the window had been left open and it was just like outside. Say, you don't suppose that that is why they can't figure out what the time of death was do you? Maybe it was like the body was stored in the refrigerator and it was preserved really good." Haydecker made the suggestion half in kidding. "I was discussing that with Plimp. He said they may even be ready to freeze people for years. But he also said that it will preserve people that are already dead."

"Cold! Of course, she could have been murdered anytime within in the previous twenty-four hours and because of the cold, and if I remember correctly, it was really cold outside during that night and day, the body wouldn't have showed the deterioration that it would have in 72 degree heat.

"Miss Haydecker, you are a genius. Why didn't I think of that." He directed that to Haydecker. Then he said, almost to himself. "That puts a whole different light on the case. I must talk to the medical examiner immediately. Now we can widen the suspects to a different time frame. We will have to go back and find out what each of the suspects was doing the twenty-four hours prior to finding the body."

Chubb happened to look down into Ozzietwo's crestfallen expression and, much to his credit, he realized immediately that Haydecker had gotten all the credit. He knew that her partner in crime, or crime-detection, had been Ozzie.

"You, too, Mr. McCaw are to be given a great deal of credit for a break-through in this case. Highly irregular it was, but at the same time I am glad you examined the empty apartment and noticed the cold temperature. This may be just what was needed." He was almost grinning to himself.

Ozzietwo puffed up at being called Mr. McCaw. He nearly fell off of the bed.

"I'll tell you what," Chubb continued. "As a reward for this great piece of detection, I will award the two of you honorary badges from Third Precinct. In addition, I will tell your parents just as little of what you have been up to as I possibly can."

Ozzietwo grinned his ear-splitting grin. Haydecker breathed a sign of relief and squeezed the arm of her partner.

"I will be back shortly. I don't know if our conversation is finished, but I must find Detective Maker and discuss this development with him. Meanwhile, the two of you stay put and keep your noses clean. The next time you two get into something like this, I will blow the whistle to your parents." Chubb walked swiftly out of the room leaving the key to Apartment 7A on the table beside the chair where he had been sitting.

Haydecker eyed it and was about to call after him. Then she closed her lips. He would probably remember it later and come back for it.

Chubb left through the front door and Haydecker flipped the lock. She looked at Ozzietwo who was lost in thought as he stared into the Wally's monitor.

"Ozzietwo, I just remembered something, while we were speaking of cold. The first time we were in the apartment, the refrigerator door was standing open, like it should be. When we leave for a vacation, the refrigerator will be off for awhile, my mom always props the door open to keep from getting bad smells.

"However, when I was in there the other afternoon the door was closed as it was today. You don't suppose someone put something else in the refrigerator to hide it?"

"Get serious, Airkool. Where would you hide something in a refrigerator that wouldn't be found right away?" Watson stared at Hercule. His eyes got wider and wider.

Are you thinking, Airkool, that we ought to have another look in that apartment in that refrigerator?" He looked pointedly at the key that had been left behind. He, too, had thought of telling Chubb. But only thought it.

"Exactly, Watson, exactly my thought. One more little look won't hurt and may certainly cast some light on this very interesting case. It is too bad that Detective Chubb had to go before we could suggest this possibility to him. Now, we will just have to follow it up on our own."

"Haydecker, we just got out of one mess!"

"We have a duty to perform, Watson! Is there any activity in the foyer?

"Airkool, it looks like 'go' to me!"

And so, the two fearless detectives once again started out to do some detecting, key in hand, they once again opened the door to the Haydecker's apartment and stepped into an empty foyer.

"Let's move it, Haydecker." Ozzietwo forgot his detective status.

Haydecker had the key in hand and more quietly than their teachers at Pelham would have ever thought possible, the two crossed the hall, slipped the key into the lock and smoothly slid into the open doorway of 7A.

"Gees, Haydecker, I mean, Airkool, are we ever getting good at this!

"Well, aren't we, Watson. How come you decided to partake of the fun? I thought you were getting cold feet? This is just a hunch I have, but I feel too silly to tell the Lieutenant that I suspect something in the refrigerator. Since he left the key, he can hardly blame us for checking, can he?"

"Sure he can, Haydecker. He can blame us a lot. And no, I am not getting cold feet. When we get caught, you get most of the blame anyway. I'll just pretend you were leading me astray."

"Some pal you are, Oz, letting me take the rap."

"Aw, you know I wouldn't do that Haydecker. We're in this together. Let check the frig."

The refrigerator door was closed just as Haydecker had remembered it from her second visit. The light did not go on when she opened the door so she assumed that the whole unit was unplugged. The door should have been standing open. Mr. Bonomolo was experienced enough as a manager of apartments to know that the odors would remain if the unit were left closed.

They opened the door. Ozzietwo peeked in. It looked like a perfectly ordinary refrigerator. Ozzietwo swung open the door to the freezer on top. He was just at eye level. To make sure, he put his arm in and felt all along the floor of the freezer.

"Nope, nothing there. Do you see anything, Haydecker?"

"No, just to make sure I will feel along the sides and top and see if anything could be taped in here. It would sure help if we had some light in the thing."

Haydecker checked the top sides of the freezer while Ozzie started to work on the other part.

"Don't look like there is anything here." He pulled out the drawer marked Crisper. It too was empty. Likewise, he checked the drawer marked Meats. He slammed the drawers back in.

"Aw, Haydecker, this is just another of your wild hairs. There isn't anything there." Ozzietwo snorted in disgust. Very un-Watson-like, his nose was running.

Haydecker stood back with her arms folded and thought for a minute.

"I was sure we were on to something." She stood and waited. "It wouldn't do any good to suppose something was behind the refrigerator. It's too big for us to move anyway."

She was about to swing the door closed. "Wait, wait just a minute, Watson. Did that sound right to you?"

"Did what sound right?" Ozzietwo had started to walk out of the kitchen.

"When you closed that drawer." She whisked over to the refrigerator again. "Do what you just did, Oz."

"Whadda ya mean, what I just did." He was being deliberately obstreperous.

"I mean open and close that last drawer. It didn't sound like the first one."

Ozzietwo bent down and pulled out first the Crisper and then Meats.

"Did you hear it, Oz." Haydecker was down on the floor before the open refrigerator.

"Yeah, I heard it. You were right, Haydecker, there is something strange about this thing. Whaddu we do?"

Haydecker was examining the drawer. She pulled it out. The same as last time, it was empty.

"You know, Oz, I think these things come all the way out of the refrigerator. Here, swing the door open wide, all the way."

The door swung back until it hit the doorway. Haydecker started to pull the Meats drawer. She pulled and slowly pulled until it separated from the slot in the bottom of the refrigerator. She turned over the drawer. The bottom was as she had expected. But, taped to the back of the drawer was a small packet of some kind of soft cloth.

"There it is, Oz, there is it."

"You found it, Haydecker, and now we will see what all this is about".

The small, black boy and the slight, white girl stood and stared at each other in front of an open refrigerator in the empty apartment. At that moment, they each wished they were some place else.

"Do you think we should open it?" Ozzietwo's voice was very small

Haydecker looked at him a long time.

"Well, how are we gonna know what to do with it if we don't know what is in it. We would feel pretty silly going to Chubb and Sam if there is nothing but junk in here."

"It seems to me that in a murder investigation, even junk can be important."

Sometimes Ozzietwo could make pretty good sense.

They stood and stared at each other some more.

"Let's do something, Haydecker, besides stand here with our fingers in our noses. I say we open it before turning it over to Chubb. Or better yet, let's open it and then put it back and forget that we ever saw it or were in this awful apartment. Again!"

"Here, you hold this a minute while I put the drawer back in the refrigerator, just in case." Haydecker handed Ozzietwo the package and tried hard in her haste not to bang the drawer against the sides of the refrigerator.

"Just in case 'what", Haydecker?" Ozzietwo was skeptical.

"Just in case, 'case', that's what. Now shut up, Ozzietwo before I bop you one. You're making me nervous."

"The only reason you're nervous is because you are getting into trouble all over again. Heck, we just got a stay of execution from Chubb and here we are in hot water again."

"OK, Oz, OK, just as soon as we look inside, we will put them back and forget we were over here."

Haydecker grabbed the package from Ozzietwo and laid it on the kitchen counter top. Carefully unrolling it, it seemed like there were miles of material before they came to the end.

Then, scattered in the center of the black cloth was a lot of white glass, rough but occasionally catching the light from the living room.

"Aw, Haydecker, it is just some broken glass. Why would anyone roll them up in a piece of cloth like that?"

"A better question, Ozzie, is why would anyone hide a bunch of broken glass in a refrigerator in an empty apartment?" Haydecker continued to stare at the shards of glass. She went on, "Oz, take one of these pieces over to the window in the living room and look at it carefully."

Ozzietwo looked at her doubtfully and then picked it up and slowly crossed into the living room and stood by the window. He held up the glass.

"Draw the sharp end of it across the window glass," Haydecker instructed.

Ozzietwo did was he was bid. A long scratch was left on the window.

Suddenly he turned on his heel. "I been askin' some stupid questions, ain't I, Haydecker?" Ozzietwo's language had a tendency to degenerate when he got excited. His mouth had dropped open and his eyes were big.

He turned back to the window. "What we are looking at is definitely not glass, is that what you are trying to tell me, Airkool?"

"You got it, Watson. The only thing that makes sense is that somehow we have stumbled onto the loot to a robbery or a smuggling operation. And someone on the 7th floor is involved or at least someone in the Towers who knows that this apartment is empty. Now, what? Oh, Oz, we've gone and done it again!"

Oz grinned at Haydecker from the window across the room. "Hey, Haydecker, haven't we though!"

"Well, great detectives that we are, I think we had better concentrate on getting rid of this loot and getting our bodies out of here pronto. We are probably holding hundreds of thousands of dollars of contraband. It is the kind of thing that people get murdered for as we have already seen. We have had enough close calls as it is."

Ozzietwo started across the room and stopped dead in his tracks. "I hear someone in the foyer. Quick, Haydecker, let's leave."

"Too late, Oz," Haydecker whispered. "We'll just have to head for the closet again." She was frantically trying to roll the cloth packet up again neatly while starting for the small bedroom. She grabbed Ozzietwo's hand on the way by and nearly threw him into the open closet door.

A key was softly sounding in the lock at the front door. It was like replaying a tape.

As before, the two persons, and there were two, because they were holding a conversation, were talking so low that Haydecker could not distinguish any of the words of their conversation. They headed directly for the kitchen and Ozzietwo and Haydecker could hear the whoosh of the refrigerator door and the rasping of metal on plastic the drawer slid out.

It was dark in the closet, and they were huddled in the shadow of the darkest corner. A slit of the light came in where the door wasn't closed tight. Haydecker was glad for that little bit of light and she was glad for the company of Ozzietwo this time. Although she was having a few pangs of regret that she had involved him in all of this.

Haydecker put her arm around Ozzietwo's shoulders. He hung on to her free hand and they listened. It seemed like there was no breathing going on inside the closet.

"Kids, I bet it was those damn kids!" A heavy male voice spoke loudly this time. Haydecker was hoping that someone was in the foyer and would wonder why the voice was coming from this apartment.

"You should have done something about it yesterday. I told you it wasn't a good idea to leave them here."

"I thought with attacking and tying up the woman that it would scare everyone else off, including those two brats who seem to stick their noses into everything. I nearly got caught this morning and I had to cosh the doorman over the head to keep from being recognized."

"Let's face it, General, this has been a botched job from beginning to end."

Suddenly, Haydecker put a face with the other voice. Of course, the voice that she had heard the first time she hid in the closet and one of the men in the kitchen was General Cargill. No wonder he had been so worried about whether she and Ozzietwo were in school. They were really getting in the way of his criminal plans.

"Maybe they are still here. Let's have a look around the apartment. I didn't see them come or go any where this afternoon."

"Nonsense, of course, they aren't still in here. They have probably gone straight to the police with the stones. I know one thing for certain, you cannot go back to your apartment. You run the risk of being caught. Perhaps, we are both in a trap right now.

"It would certainly be helpful to find those children. If nothing else we could use them as hostages for safe passage out of the country."

"I'd like it if we could just get out of this building, much less out of the country. I am against taking hostages. This has gone way too far now, Andres." It was the General talking.

"This is no time for you to be getting cold feet. We did what we had to do when we killed the girl. If necessary, we will take those children with us and dispose of them at a convenient time. We probably should have disposed of them long ago." Andres was speaking in his thickly accent voice and to Haydecker it was the most menacing thing she had ever heard. Somehow when they talked like that on TV, it didn't sound quite so dangerous.

"Come, have a look around." The voice got louder and nearer.

"I tell you, it is a wild goose chase. They have escaped back into one of their apartments." The footsteps grew louder on the bare floor of the bedroom. Haydecker had just time to wedge the packet into the crack of the door as it opened.

Bright light blinded them as the door swung open.

"Well, look what we have here. A couple of wild geese just ready to be plucked." The General grabbed Haydecker by an arm and Ozzietwo by an arm and hauled them roughly out of their hiding place. He held Ozzietwo so high his feet didn't even touch the ground.

"So, who have the two of you told about what you found here? Have you seen the detectives? Tell the truth, now, and no lying or it will go hard with you as it did with our blonde friend from

Amsterdam. She didn't tell the whole truth. Now she is in a position to tell no truths at all."

"Cargill, quit talking to those children and find out where the stones are. We are not interested in teaching object lessons to a couple of spoiled American children."

Haydecker thought she would much rather deal with the General than she would with Andres. He seemed the blood- thirsty type. Unfortunately, she and Ozzietwo just happened to have dropped by. He wasn't being very hospitable.

The General let go of Haydecker's arm and grabbed Ozzietwo's other one and held Oz aloft until the two were face to face. Ozzietwo was ashy pale and the General's face was red with anger and frustration.

"All right, young man, tell me where the two of you put those stones and you had better tell me right now. Don't lie or beat about the bush."

"What stones?" Haydecker was proud of Ozzietwo for giving it the old try no matter how scared he was. "I haven't seen any stones."

"Unfortunately, I don't believe you. The fact that you were on the scene today is almost certain evidence. Now you must have hidden them someplace else. Where?" He shook Ozzietwo, hard.

Haydecker felt like she, herself, was jolted.

"Quit fooling around with him, General. Hang him out the window by one foot. It is sure to loosen his tongue. If it doesn't, we can just drop him and say that he was playing in the empty apartment and had an accident. We don't have to get blamed for this one."

The General put Ozzietwo down. Ozzie looked to Haydecker like he was on the verge of tears but his mouth was sealed in a straight line. He looked the part of the hard-bitten detective when the game was up.

The man called Andres, still wearing that too-long black overcoat, shoved General Cargill aside and grabbed Ozzietwo by the back of the belt and turned him upside down.

Haydecker, who had been momentarily forgotten with the focus on Ozzietwo, decided in that split second that it had gone far enough. "Stop! Put him down! I will tell you where the diamonds are. Let him go!"

Andres dropped Ozzietwo with a thump and turned on Haydecker. He approached her menacingly. His pale green eyes were focused intently on her. Haydecker remembered later thinking that his eyes were the coldest eyes she had ever seen. She shivered involuntarily.

"Go, Oz, now!" Haydecker used the moment that Andres attention was turned on her to yell at Ozzietwo. She saw Ozzietwo shake his head to clear the cobwebs. She knew he was thinking when she saw him start to edge toward the door.

"Cargill, don't let the boy escape! I will work on the girl."

But the General was slower than Ozzietwo and he also wasn't as frightened. Ozzietwo broke for the door, his tennis-shoed feet flying. Haydecker held her breath a moment as his 10 year-old fingers fumbled at the doorknob. General Cargill caught up to him and grabbed the back of his sweatshirt. Ozzietwo had the door open and, wiggling and squirming, managed to worm his way out of the too-big sweatshirt. The General was left holding a handful of material and Ozzietwo was "gone."

The General slammed the door shut and both locked and bolted it. He stormed back into the apartment, his face red and glaring from underneath his bushy white eyebrows. He was breathing hard.

However, at that particular moment, Haydecker wasn't too concerned about the General's eyebrows. The man called Andres had grabbed a hold of her by the hair on the back of her neck and was pulling hard. Haydecker would remember the overwhelming experience that Anders' breath reeked like a wild animal.

"Where are they, Mademoiselle, and you had better be quick about it. It matters not that your little, black friend has disappeared. You are with us, you, who know where the diamonds are and who will be our passport out of this building."

Muffled by the closed door and the walls, but nonetheless, clear enough to be heard, Haydecker could hear Ozzietwo bellowing, "HELP, POLICE, HELP, HELP!" Haydecker was sure that everyone in the building, in the city, on this side of the state would not miss that call for rescue. Bless Ozzietwo! At least he was safe, and would not get hurt because she had been so silly as to want to return to 7A.

She could see no reason in prolonging the situation. Her hair hurt where Andres was pulling it and she thought she might at any moment throw-up. It was a combination of the stench of Andres' breath and the fact that her stomach was rolling over and over from being locked in the empty apartment with two killers.

"They are in the closet, wedged in the door by the hinge."

"They'd better be there." Andres gave her hair an extra yank and then let it go and moved swiftly to the closet where he knelt on the floor inside, only his black-coated rear-end visible from the door.

Haydecker had a brief, only brief, notion to kick it. For a change, her better sense ruled her behavior.

The General had rushed over to the closet door. "Are they there?"

Andres didn't answer but backed out of the closet, clutching the black wrapped package in his hand. He took it directly to the kitchen counter top to unroll it, just as Haydecker had done.

"You see if you can hang on to the girl until we decide what is to be done," Andres ordered the General. The General, quickly obeying, grabbed Haydecker's arm, rather harder than Haydecker thought was necessary. But then, the General had already had one bad experience.

The General then let go of her arm. She wondered if she dare make a run for it. Neither the General or Andres appeared to be either young or quick, but the door was not only locked but also bolted. Ozzietwo had not had to release the bolt. It would take too much time. She stood quietly and waited.

"They look to be all there." Andres sniffed in satisfaction as he looked at the diamonds. The General didn't respond but also looked satisfied as he stared down at the glittering pile on the black cloth. Haydecker still thought they looked like glass.

"Well, the next problem is getting out of here." The General seemed tired when he spoke. Haydecker reflected that he was no spring chicken and was probably not used to the strenuous activity of playing cops and robbers.

Andres looked up from his contemplation of the stones and remarked, "I suppose that young idiot boy has bellowed our whereabouts all over the building. I suppose it is too much to ask for that he would consider that his friend's life would be in danger if he went to the police."

Andres had no more than gotten the words out when there was a pounding on the door. Ozzietwo had gotten the word out and fast.

"We know you are in there." It sounded like Chubb's voice but it was muffled enough so that Haydecker couldn't be sure. "Come out now, give us the girl unhurt, and we will do what we can to see that the courts deal leniently with you."

The two men, dragging Haydecker along, moved over to the vicinity of the door where they could hear and be heard more clearly. Andres placed Haydecker right in front of the door. He and the General stood off to one side.

"Sorry, Inspector, but that is not apt to be a story that we will accept. You have no powers to deal with the courts. Besides, at this time you have no evidence against us. It is all circumstantial."

"If you don't let that child go this moment, we have you on kidnapping charges. I am sure your friend, the General, can inform you that penalties in this state for kidnapping are harsh, especially for kidnapping children."

Haydecker didn't like being referred to as a child, although she supposed she was. She also mused that who better to kidnap than a kid. For that she certainly qualified.

"Miss Haydecker, " it was surely Silent Sam this time, "are you all right?"

Before Haydecker could answer another voice piped up, "Speak to me, Airkool, or I will beat the door down." Who else but her companion in detection, Watson.

"I'm OK. Congratulations on your escape, Watson! You will certainly get a medal . . ."

Andres clapped his hand over her mouth. "That's enough! I will do the talking," he hissed at Haydecker.

Then to the closed door and whomever might be on the other side, "Remain certain, we have no intention of walking out of here and turning ourselves over to the police. Remember, we have a hostage who is our passport out of here. Listen carefully, Lieutenant. I will give you instructions."

Haydecker's heart sank. She somehow had known that it wasn't going to be so easy as just walking out the door to freedom.

She looked at the General; he didn't look any too well. He was sweating a lot and his color was all wrong. Beads of moisture dotted his forehead .

Haydecker wondered if he was afraid or if something was really wrong.

Another voice spoke up from beyond the door, "Scarecrow, it's dad, don't pull any heroics—do what they say!"

Oh, no, her dad had had to come home. Now the fat was really in the fire.

Dimly, she could hear Ozzietwo bellow, "Scarecrow? That's a good one! I never heard that before." Airkool wondered if she would ever see Watson again. Things were certainly looking bleak.

Chapter XVI

Haydecker could scarcely breathe with Andres' hand over her mouth. She had tried wiggling but he held her all the more tightly. She needed to save her energy and think. She was trying hard to think.

The General was leaning against the wall. A film of perspiration covered his brow and he was struggling hard to make his breath come evenly. Just seeing him sweat made Haydecker feel better. Obviously he wasn't all that good at this crime stuff.

"Listen, carefully," a voice, loud, but calm and reassuring, at least to Haydecker, came through the door. "Let us exchange the girl for another hostage; there is no sense in risking the life of a child too."

Haydecker resented all this child stuff, but if it would make Andres and the General back off, she was all for it.

Andres answered back quickly, "There is every reason, Lieutenant; this is the Lieutenant, isn't it? She is small, she is biddable, and will be easily be managed. We are not worried that you will shoot us. You would not risk hitting her. No, Lieutenant, she will do perfectly fine as a hostage. There is much at stake here. We will take the best chance we can."

A high voice bellowed, "Hey, Haydecker, hang tough. You can handle 'em." It was, of course, Ozzietwo, also known in some parts as Watson, the Wonderful.

Haydecker wondered why they hadn't banished him to his apartment. Then, she realized that he was valuable for explaining what had gone on inside the apartment. She realized, too, that he was invaluable to raise her spirits. And right now she really needed some heavy-duty spirit raising. She wasn't so biddable!

Andres continued, "Please have ready for us a car at the front door in fifteen minutes. Have ready for us at the airport, a plane with ample fuel for a trans-Atlantic flight and a crew. Then, clear the foyer and the stairwell. When I open that door, I want no one visible, not even peeking out a door. Remember, both the General and I have guns. It is obvious by now that we are not afraid to use them."

"When will you release the hostage?" It was Silent Sam being unsilent.

"When we decide. Get started immediately. You have only 14 minutes left. Enough talking." Andres dragged Haydecker back into the living room as he looked at his watch.

Haydecker could hear only dull murmurings in the background outside the door and outside the window in the street seven floors below. Inside the apartment, the General was continuing to breathe in short gasps through his mouth. Haydecker wondered idly if he were about to have a heart attack or something. His mouth worked as though he wanted to say something but nothing came out. He continued to lean up against the wall.

Andres watched his compatriot for a moment and then, snapped at him, his accented voice sending shivers down Haydecker's spine, "General, I cannot have anything further go wrong with this operation. Don't become ill, because if you do I will leave you here. If only one of us can escape with the diamonds, that one will be me at any sacrifice. If you are able to come that is fine; if you don't, that is also fine."

The General finally spoke, "I agreed to this operation, including the theft and smuggling. But at no time did I agree to murder, either of an adult or a child. One death is enough and now, there is no need make the situation worse." The General's military manner had disappeared. He seemed just like everyone else now.

"Neither of us knew it would come to this. But you knew that when we were playing for such high stakes, that anything was possible. Elise's death was all part of the operation. And if this child must be sacrificed, so be it. She shouldn't have been so curious about what was going on. Children should not be heard from."

Andres loosened his hand from Haydecker's mouth and grabbed onto her wrist, twisting and forcing her to sit down along the wall.

Nothing more was said for a few minutes. Andres stood quietly listening to what was happening in the hall and darting to the window every few minutes to look down to the street below. General Cargill continued to stand against the wall. He seemed to be breathing a little better, although, Haydecker thought, she was no expert on breathing. Right now she didn't feel like much of an expert on anything. She had really screwed things up. How glad she was the Ozzietwo had escaped and wasn't trapped in here due to her stupidity.

Finally, Andres took one last look at his watch, a heavy piece of metal, Haydecker thought, practically big enough to be on a spaceship or maybe a coo-coo clock. He moved from the window to the door, saying to the General on his way by, "Keep an eye on the girl while I finish these preparations."

The General barely looked at Haydecker who was still sitting against the wall where she had been forced down. She wanted to assure him that she wasn't about to make a break for it, but she certainly wasn't going to give him that satisfaction.

Andres put his mouth near the paneling of the door, "Lieutenant, Lieutenant, the time is up! Are you ready with the arrangements. I can't see a car outside the window."

"Keep calm. The car is on its way. These things cannot be accomplished so quickly."

"You will be surprised how quickly things can be accomplished when there is a life at stake, Lieutenant."

"Let us speak to Miss Haydecker for a moment. After all, this whole escape is predicated on hostage safety."

Andres motioned at Haydecker with his gun, "Get up and come over here. Say something to the Lieutenant."

Haydecker got up slowly even though she wanted to move faster. She felt like a hundred and three. What's more, she couldn't think of anything to say. Chubb and Sam must be really furious with her and Oz for not staying out of trouble.

"Speak!" Andres snapped at her like ordering a dog to obedience.

She wanted to lean up to the door and go "Arf, arf," and the thought of that made her want to giggle and giggle. Why, at this most serious moment in her life, did she keep wanting to laugh?

"This is Emily." Her own voice surprised her. It was thin and high. She didn't sound anything like herself at all.

"Haydecker!" It was Ozzietwo sounding loud, very loud, and very much like himself. "You OK? Do you want me to come back in there with you?" Surrounded by cops, Ozzietwo sounded pretty brave.

There was some hushing and shushing on the other side of the door and then faintly Haydecker could hear, "Well, she's my friend and my partner. I'll speak to her if I want to. She'll tell me more stuff than she will you."

Andres bellowed out, "Get that other child out of there. One of the small monsters is enough to contend with."

"I'm OK, Watson." She felt better just having heard Ozzietwo's voice. He had that effect on one.

The voice of Chubb broke in before Haydecker could say any more, "The car is ready, and by the time you get to the airport, the plane will be fueled and provisioned and ready to go. I am asking again. Will you let us exchange hostages with you? Miss Haydecker for Sgt. Walker?"

"Leave things as they are, Lieutenant. Now clear the hall."

"Will you be using the elevator or the stairs?"

"Your job, Lieutenant, is to stay out of sight until that car pulls away from the curb. Do not worry about how we will get downstairs."

There was rustling outside the door. Andres looked out the peep hole and then turned around to give a malevolent stare at the General who was standing where he had been since the exchange began.

"Cargill, will you come or do you insist on being left behind?"

"I'll come." The General was as white as the wall he was standing next to.

"Good, don't let the operation down again. I will let the girl lead us out the door. I will keep the gun to her head at all times. You follow me, but keep your back to mine and keep your gun drawn. If you see anyone, anything, any movement, don't hesitate to shoot. Remember, we have nothing to lose at this point--and everything to gain."

The General didn't say anything but moved away from the wall. "Why don't I keep an eye on the girl and you cover our rear?"

"Because, my dear General, you simply haven't got the stomach for shooting, if the task becomes necessary. We both know that. The only reason I take you with me is because I need the extra man. Fortunately, the police don't know of your lack of ability in this area, and you, a retired General too."

The General had gone from very white to a very red face. He did not respond to the goading from Andres.

Then the three of them lined up inside the door. Andres put the cold metal of the gun just along Haydecker's chin, resting it on her jaw bone.

Haydecker had to go to the bathroom. Desperately she tried to pretend she didn't and used the old trick her grandmother had taught her about pretending she was in a desert, with hot, dry sand stretching on for miles and miles. It didn't help much.

Andres gave one last scan out the peep hole and then, still holding the gun in his right hand, carefully and slowly, with his left, opened the door. He nudged Haydecker a step into the foyer while he stood in the doorway, his eyes shifting from right to left and looking down the long hall. What he saw apparently satisfied him.

"Ready, Cargill?" It was an order more than a question. When the General didn't answer, Haydecker felt Andres turn to look at his partner.

"All right, let's go." Andres was the only one saying anything. The General didn't seem to have much to say and Haydecker certainly wasn't going to risk it either saying or doing anything she wasn't told. The feel of the gun against her cheek was very persuasive.

The procession moved several steps slowly forward. Haydecker went first with Andres hand on one shoulder and the gun on the other. The smell of Andres breath was like a cloud around her. She could hear rather than see the General following. His breathing was noisy and rasping. It was like he couldn't get enough air. Haydecker knew the feeling.

Suddenly, and yet it seemed like he had been there all along, walking slowly down the hall toward them was Ozzietwo. He moved as if in slow motion. Haydecker wondered if she had fallen asleep or if this was what it was like to faint. She had heard much about fainting, but until now she had never fainted. She thought, "There is a first time for everything and that she was having too many first times today."

Haydecker noticed every detail of his clothing; he wore high-topped, black and white tennis shoes, a faded red, almost light purple sweatshirt, and always and ever Ozzietwo was in too-tight jeans.

When Andres didn't acknowledge him, Haydecker was sure that she had fainted and was wishing for Ozzie's company in some unconscious state. Then, she became aware of beads of sweat that stood out along Ozzietwo's hairline and across the bridge of his nose. It wasn't fainting if she could see Ozzie sweat.

Then, she felt Andres start at the sight of the fourth party in the hall. Haydecker was sure that it was no faint and it was no dream.

Even if everything else seemed unreal, Ozzietwo sweating was not. Because he was in a perpetual state of motion, he was usually in a perpetual state of perspiration.

"What are you doing out here. What kind of a trick is this? Don't you know you could get yourself and your friend killed with a stupid trick like this. Or, did the police put you up to this?" Andres snarled.

"No, the police don't even know I am here." Ozzietwo's voice was kind of quavery and Haydecker was in doubt as to whether he could finish the sentence. But he went on in a stronger voice, "Where Haydecker goes, I go. We are in this together." He stood glaring across some twenty feet of space at Andres. His stare, his whole body dared Andres to send him away.

All was silence in the foyer. Ozzietwo stared at Andres and Andres stared back. Silence roared. Haydecker wondered if, indeed, she was going to faint. The cold metal of the gun burned against her jawbone.

Finally, Andres spoke, "Now, Miss, tell your little black friend here to leave and leave quickly if he wants to see you get out of the building alive. He must have nothing but fuzz in his head to attempt such a trick. Tell, him."

"Listen, Oz," Haydecker wasn't sure at all that her voice was going to work. "You had better do as he said. We got you safely out of this once. Get out of here again." This time, Haydecker, sensed rather than saw, the detectives listening behind the doors in the foyer and the hall.

Suddenly there was a slight swoosh of air and a soft thump behind them. There was a "hummphing" noise. She thought for a moment that Andres had gone until she felt again the pressure of his hand on her shoulder.

Ozzie's eyes got big, almost big enough to see the reflection of the scene in the. Then he gave a whoop and a blood-curdling yell as, at top speed, he rushed toward them.

"Hit the deck, Haydecker." Reacting more in instinct than to his words, she dove for the carpet, rolling as she went. Her last sight was Ozzietwo coming in low for Andres' knees. She heard the gun hit the far wall and felt the explosion of detonation.

Suddenly, the foyer was full of policemen who had come boiling out of all the doors the minute Ozzie had let out his yell. Haydecker sat up and struggled to turn around to see what was happening and where her rescuer was in the melee on the floor.

Two policemen had grabbed Andres' arms, one on either side. Another policeman was on the floor, applying some kind of first aid to a General who was struggling to get his breath. His collapse had provided the sound effects behind her.

Ozzietwo was sitting up on his knees, breathing heavily too, but apparently all in one piece. He was watching with careful attention what was happening to the General and to Andres.

He looked over at Haydecker. He grinned. He grinned with all 28 teeth and some wisdom teeth that he didn't even have yet. He grinned with his eyes and with his ears. His whole body was smiling.

Ozzie caught her eye. "Hey, Haydecker, you OK?"

"Hey, Ozzie, I'm OK. You OK?"

"Me too." Ozzie grinned some more. Haydecker smiled right back. It seemed like she couldn't stop.

Chapter XVII

It took some days for the seventh floor at Hatterfield Towers to return to anything nearly approaching a normal schedule. Or for that matter, for certain of the residents to anywhere nearly return to their usual schedules and their usual behaviors.

Everyone seemed glad to see each other, Haydecker noticed. Tenants talked in the halls. They no longer jumped at the sight of each other. They appeared genuinely glad that the guilty party in the most recent crimes was not the person to whom they were talking.

Ozzie was in and out of the Haydecker apartment. He ran faster than usual, spoke louder than usual, and his tolerance for sitting still was almost at point zero. Haydecker had found it difficult to have a conversation with him of more than three sentences. His concentration didn't seem to last that long.

As for herself, she was glad to return to bed. While it seemed like she felt better, she was none the less having the old aches. It seemed like she liked the alone times a little more than she usually did. She speculated that maybe it was relief at having gotten out of that tight spot with no damage done.

Especially, she felt responsible for Ozzie. It was she who had encouraged him to participate in the case. And even if she hadn't encouraged him to walk heroically down the hall at the end and take a dive at Andres, she would have been responsible. Ozzie, of course, wanted to take responsibility for himself. Not that she could blame him.

It was finally the week-end and on Friday evening, when the Haydeckers and the McCaws were home, Chubb and Sam had made a final appointment to come to the Haydecker apartment after dinner to tie up loose ends.

Ozzie had come ripping in a half-hour earlier to discuss things with his former partner. It was true, though, that the detectives, Watson and Hercule or Airkool, were gone and the walkie-talkies had been put away. Haydecker thought that they would probably stay put for a while.

"Hey, Haydecker, or should I call you Emily Marie, now that you are a celebrity? I read your name in the paper and I hardly even knew it was you they are writing about." Oz was sitting in a chair for a change.

"Just be warned, Ozzie, that if you start calling me Emily Marie, I will certainly have to address you as Oswald Parsival."

"Parsival!" Ozzie hit the ceiling. "Where did you ever make up that."

"Who's to know? So, just lay off the Emily Marie stuff. If you have to call me something, I guess Emily is enough. Goodness knows I'm used to it enough from teachers and other people."

"Things are really going to be boring around here this week-end. Not really much to do. I guess solving murder cases can really get into your blood."

"Or the blood of them can get all over you. Either way, I guess I can live without it. In fact, I am sure I can. We will think of something to do this weekend, Oz. Who knows, we could even play a game of checkers or do some homework!"

Ozzie slid off of the chair and onto the floor. He picked himself up and wandered over to the window, pulling back the drapes to look out into the few streaks of the winter day that were left in the sky.

"So, what else is new? Anything happened at school today?" Ozzie was certainly not himself.

He stared outside a few minutes without saying anything. And then, without turning, he began, "Do you remember, Haydecker, when we went into the apartment the last time. You gave me a diamond and sent me over to the window to check it out."

"Geez, Oz, how could I forget." It seemed like every moment of that time in the apartment had been made into a video and it played over and over in her head. Plainly, she was tired of all the reruns.

"Well, well," finally Oz turned around and started approaching the bed with a curious limping gait. He was trying to get his hand into the back pocket of his jeans while walking at the same time.

"Here, Haydecker, do you remember this piece of glass." There in Ozzie's brownish-pink palm was one of the more sizeable diamonds. She remembered that she had picked it from the pile because it would be big enough for him to hang on to when he tried it on the window glass.

"Some glass, huh?" Haydecker smiled ruefully.

"I forgot I had it in the excitement of the capture on Wednesday night. Then, today, I put these jeans on again. At school, I reached into the pocket, and there it was. Cripes, what do you think it is worth?"

"Once it is cut, a lot, I guess."

"What should we do with it? Do we dare keep it? They sure won't ever miss it. But I guess we would know, wouldn't we?" Ozzie made a wry face.

"Yeah, we'd know. And someday we'd have to dispose of it, somehow. Maybe we could have it made into a ring for your dearly beloved."

"Shut up, Haydecker. I am not ever gonna have one of those."

"I think the best thing to do it turn it over to Chubb tonight. Let's get rid of this whole thing. I don't want anything hanging over my head."

"I guess you are right, Haydecker. We do have a prize from the police. I guess not everyone has Precinct Badges. Although I don't suppose I will be wearing it much."

"Sometimes we can get them out, Oz, and remember what happened. But not very soon. That's for darn sure!"

"Oh, come on, Haydecker. Admit that you had a little fun."

"Sure, I'll admit it Oz- - -in between the scary parts, like seeing the dead body on the foyer floor, and being in that dark apartment, and, for that matter, being in the light apartment with those two thugs."

Ozzie's eyes were beginning to light up. He seemed to remember the whole experience with more pleasure than Haydecker. "Finding the note in the plant and you finding the purse in the closet, and finally finding the loot."

"Oz, the worst part of all, for me, was looking down that hall and seeing you coming. I wanted to tell you to go back. Yet you kept coming."

Ozzietwo's chest was beginning to puff out a little, "Aw, Haydecker, he wasn't gonna kill you or me. The police would have sliced him up into little bits. Remember that the murder of the Elise girl was an accident. In spite of how tough he talked, Andres, and the General too, weren't all that much Rambo types."

"I couldn't believe it when you charged him!"

"Well, when I saw the General go down. I just kept thinking how easy it would be to topple Andres over backwards, flipping his legs out from under him."

"It was, easy, I mean. I thought at any moment I would lose my head.

Maybe you were right, and they wouldn't shoot."

"I guess we were lucky I was right!"

The front door buzzer rang and Wally's monitor revealed Mr. and Mrs. McCaw standing in the foyer and just getting off of the elevator were Chubb and Silent Sam. Mrs. Haydecker answered the door.

"Time to go, Airkool."

"Coming, Watson." The two detectives went to write the final chapter.

The meeting in the Haydecker living room was very formal and Haydecker felt grown-up. She hadn't had a dress on in months. She could tell Ozzie felt grown-up, too. They even each drank coffee, awful-tasting stuff, while eating the little cookies that Emily's mother had prepared. Of course, Ozzie could demolish 10 or 12 of those little puppies without even chewing hard.

Mr. and Mrs. McCaw sat on the couch with Ozzie between them. The others were arranged in occasional chairs throughout the room. Woof leaned his head against Haydecker's knee and made a low noise of affection and contentment. Haydecker had insisted that he be allowed to come.

Chubb held the floor, explaining to the Haydecker's and the McCaw's any details that they did not already know. There were even a few things that Emily Marie and Oswald were not up on. Chubb was in his glory.

"There are just a few odds and ends we need to explain to you all before we can call this case closed."

Ozzie piped in, "I have a little odd and end to take care of too."

"Good, then let's get started." Chubb helped himself to one of Mrs. Haydecker's delicious frosted chocolate cookies.

"You are probably wondering how the General is doing? He, as Mrs. Haydecker probably knows, will be out of intensive care soon. But, we don't know how soon he will be able to stand trial. Or even if. His heart attack was pretty severe.

"Do you mean he might get to remain free in spite of all his crimes, robbery, kidnapping, accessory to murder, there is quite a list?" Mrs. McCaw was aghast. The General had not been a favorite with the ladies on the floor, such as Golda, and Mrs. McCaw or even the Misses Gerot and Onken.

"It will depend. He has to be tried in the courts and his lawyer may convince the judge he cannot go to trial. The other fellow is wanted both here and in Amsterdam for crimes. I guess they will make some international agreement about him.

"At any rate it was a stroke of luck for us, especially for Emily, that he had the heart attack when he did. However, if it hadn't been for Oswald's quick action, it might not have ended so well. It was a rash thing you did, young man!" Chubb looked sternly at Ozzie.

Chubb no longer intimidated Ozzie. Ozzie sat there on the stuffed sofa. Haydecker could see that he was just itching to bounce on it. There were no outward signs. She could just tell. After you had a friend for a long time, you could just tell.

Ozzie asked, "Didn't they really murder that dead girl."

"Well, yes and no. That was the last thing they really wanted to do was murder their courier. She was killed accidentally when Andres was trying to scare her. It led to all sorts of complications including the unraveling of the whole case.

"Where was she murdered?" It was Mr. Haydecker, more relaxed now, asking the question.

"They were only supposed the be using the empty apartment for a brief while on that Sunday late afternoon and Sunday night, knowing that Mr. Bonomolo would not be likely to be showing it to any prospective tenants on a Sunday evening. Unfortunately, Elise was murdered during the afternoon. They opened the windows until they could decide what to with the body and then they stashed the smuggled stones in the refrigerator. They thought that in case the body was discovered, it would be better if they weren't caught with any damaging evidence on their persons or in the General's apartment."

The doorbell buzzed. Mr. Haydecker covered the few steps from his chair to the door quickly. It was Mad Harold standing there with a grin on his face. "Mr. Bonomolo said I should come on up for this post mortem since things are considerably quieter around here now that Ozzie has nabbed all the criminals." He winked at Oz. Another chair was brought and Harold was quickly seated.

"Well, why did they leave the body in the hall?" Mr. McCaw questioned when Harold had been seated.

"That has been very difficult to piece together. It was a little bit like a comedy movie here on Sunday evening and Sunday night. I guess the plan was to move the body up to the rooftop. It might be some time before it was discovered up there, especially in the winter. Then, too, the seventh floor would not be pinpointed as a location for the action."

"Was that what was going on when I couldn't get the elevator to work when I came in from the airport on Sunday night?" Mrs. Haydecker remembered her troubles with the elevator stopping at the wrong floor.

"The plan was to stop the elevator and carry her up to the roof. If the elevator wouldn't stop on seventh, they couldn't be surprised by anyone coming onto the floor as they were carrying the body. I really don't know why they didn't wait until later for their first try."

"Is that why the General walked up the stairs on Sunday night? Everyone thought he was crazy. It is funny he didn't have his attack then!"

"He was supposed to be the decoy and the advance man. It obviously didn't work. Later that night, toward morning, they tried again. This time they didn't stop the elevator and Grace Onken came home late from a date and surprised them. Except she didn't know she had. At first, that is. Later on she realized that she had seen something because she had run into the General in the hall. She just hadn't put two and two together."

"Was that why she came to see me?" Haydecker piped up.

"She was just going to scout around and see if you knew anything. She was doubly afraid, both of the General and then of us, since she had been so long in coming forth."

"Do you know that message in the plant, the one that Oz and I didn't show to you because we didn't tell you about the man dressed in black? We finally figured it out."

Chubb gave a snort. "Do you know how much this whole thing might have been simplified if you had shared that little bit of information with the police department? Let's hear what you came up with as far as breaking the code."

"Oz and I decided that that numbers merely stood for the time of a meeting and the date: 2200 stood for ten o'clock, especially since that's the way the General would have talked in the military; the 1 was for January and 28 was for the day."

"Good for you! By the time we had the message it was past the 28th. It is too bad you didn't work on it before. However, maybe it is a good thing. The two of you would have had to decide to go to the meeting." Chubb gave a sigh. "We might have had another disaster!"

Harold had been pretty quiet. "What I really want to know, Lieutenant, is who else did you suspect and why?"

"Well, Simpson, according to regulations, I suppose I should tell you that everyone was a suspect. Let me assure you that it wasn't true. At no time did I suspect young McCaw here. Were you a suspect? Sure, and most of the adults in the building. There were a couple of strange behaviors reported that we had to check up on that were like wild goose chases. For example, Mr. and Mrs. Mohr have been having some of the usual newlywed difficulties and Mr. Mohr, in an effort to make her jealous, has been deliberately staying out late."

Ozzie had been pretty quiet through most of Chubb's speech, but he finally leaned over to Haydecker in his loudest whisper, "Did we ever find out what was in his/her shoe out there in the foyer?"

"What's this?" Chubb and Silent Sam both were instantly at attention.

"When Andres was out in the foyer dressed as the old woman. . ." Haydecker was interrupted.

"He took something out of his size 50 wedgies." Ozzie erupted into giggles. Haydecker couldn't help smiling herself.

"I guess that is something we'll never know. As you might guess, Andres is not too helpful with the details. And now, Oswald, you have something you wanted to say."

Ozzie wiggled and wiggled trying to get his hand into his pocket. Then he opened his fist and, just as Haydecker had remembered it, there, looking like it had grown, was the uncut diamond.

"When we got surprised by the General and Andres, I had it in my hand. Haydecker rolled up the rest of the diamonds so fast, I just stuck it in my pocket."

"Thank you, Mr. McCaw, for being so honest. And that brings me to the last item of business." He took a small item out of his suit pocket and Silent Sam, without having to be told, did likewise.

"As you know, those of us on the Detective Force are not able to accept gifts of appreciation. However, Miss Haydecker and Mr. McCaw the second, are not regulars on our force even though you have received honorary badges. And the two of us are willing to admit that while you made this case harder at times, you also did a portion of the work. Certainly the dangerous parts were yours."

"Therefore, on behalf of The House VanDaam, the diamond wholesalers, from whom all those stones were stolen, they have asked us to give you each a little reward. They are probably more appropriate for when you have grown up a little more." He handed a box each to Haydecker and Ozzie.

Ozzie tore into his. Haydecker tried to be a little more dignified.

Ozzie's mouth became an "O" and his eyes widened as he looked down at the gold and diamond cuff links.

Haydecker opened her box. Suspended at the end of a golden chain was a single diamond. It caught the light in the living room and seemed to sparkle everywhere.

Emily Marie Haydecker, holding a diamond necklace, looked over at Ozwald McCaw II, holding a pair of diamond cuff links. They smiled at each other in amazement, agreement and relief and a few assorted other things.

"Well, Oz, I guess we had better get started growing up so we can wear these. Hey, Ozzietwo, it will be something we will remember, won't it?

Ozzie gave his partner and his friend the thumbs up sign. "Hey, Haydecker. Won't it ever!" At least until we can spot another mystery lurking on the 7th floor.

Chapter XVIII

Emily Marie Haydecker and Oswald McCaw, also known in local environs as Airkool and Watson, suspend their detecting activities to spend time on school. They do keep on the alert just in case they should stumble on another opportunity to solve crime. . .

Ann Boultinghouse Bio

I think I was born writing. It is kind of natural, like eating or breathing. I probably had a pen or pencil in my hand yelling at the birth doctor to give me some paper. Having been there, you will understand that it is no place for a copy book, a computer or an iPad.

Since that time I have done all sorts of writing, some of it OK and some of it wretched. My earliest memory is as a third-grader penning or penciling a most astonishing one-act play entitled, "When the Wind Whistled." I don't remember much about the plot other than it was supposed to be scary and the rain and wind were major to the story line. In third grade, I also started my first novel about twins who went to the Kentucky Derby. There were some good things about cleaning out the attic when I grew up. Those pieces disappeared. My mother thought I was funny and weird trying to be a writer. I have not forgiven her, even when I knew these efforts weren't close to being good. What did I know?

I went from being a dramatist to working on the *Tatler*, the high school newspaper, and the yearbook. I wrote an original oration and became an extemporaneous speaker at Iowa High School Speech Program and got high marks at their contests. I continued to produce very bad poetry, which was published here and there including the poetry anthology, *Lyrical Iowa*. Also some of it was published in the church bulletin. Perhaps that explains my somewhat uncomfortable relationship with my maker.

After I became a teacher, it was difficult to find time to write and so I did it sporadically. I would start a book and then lose interest and abandon it. Mostly, when I wrote I would set time limits or page limits, which would keep the project going. The quality was sacrificed when a day had to be skipped because I would have to grade papers or essays or plan lessons. Family issues would intervene and I would have to put it aside for a while. The worst damage would be done when I tried to write in the classroom when the students were attending to their own assignments, unprofessional and nonproductive.

There were other short writing stints such as being a newsletter contributor when I was a board member and president of the Iowa Talented and Gifted Association (ITAG), which tried to make contact with both parents and teachers of gifted students. I was also invited to take a part-time job as a grant writer for the educational agency after I retired. I did like the writing; I didn't so much mind the research, but I hated above all things making the cold calls to these philanthropic foundations and groups that had money to give. It turned out I was successful at grant writing but I didn't last long.

I also wrote and published some educational materials. I love doing this. I wrote *The Poetry Box,* which was published by Educational Insights. I was published in an educational magazine for an article on "LoldiGocks and the Pee Thrigs." I did some research on learning styles of primary students and compiled my findings and it found a publisher in *The Roeper Review.*

Upon retirement I found myself with about four novels, all of them awful, which I hadn't the heart to rewrite now that I had the time and some direction. It was wonderful when the computer came on the scene and I learned to compose at the computer, which provided an opportunity for immediate corrections. What was really hard was doing full-scale editing and getting rid of writing. It was traumatic to destroy the wonderful things I had written—even when I knew they weren't— wonderful, that is.

Browse other books written by Ann Boultinghouse on the
Amazon Kindle Platform

Confessions of a Teach – A - Holic

Like Children Collecting Pebbles

26112168R00113

Printed in Great Britain
by Amazon